Dreaming Eli

by

JoMarie DeGioia

PUBLISHED BY:

Bailey Park Publishing

Copyright © JoMarie DeGioia 2016

ISBN: 978-1-944181-08-6

Dreaming Eli

Book Seven of the
Cypress Corners Series

by

JoMarie DeGioia

Chapter 1

Chapman Financial, Boston

Elijah Graham turned his chair to face the mammoth expanse of glass behind his desk. He could only see sky from his vantage point, that and the other high rises bracketing Bill Chapman's monument to himself. He couldn't see the streets far below, but even if he could they wouldn't be the streets he'd known growing up. No. This place was far from that hell, thank God. There were even trees lining the streets down there, their leaves just starting to turn.

As the top guy in Sales and Account Retention at Chapman, Eli had his finger on the pulse of their clients' needs and wants. He could hone in on their desires, and say just what was necessary to lock them down and close the deal. Being in and out of foster homes since he was three years old, he knew all about speaking and acting in just the perfect way to fit in. To please. To stay, although that last one never quite seemed to stick.

"Eli," Bill Chapman boomed, stalking into Eli's office.

Eli was used to his brusqueness. Bill never gave more than a terse greeting, and Eli often wondered if there was any softness beneath the man's gruff exterior.

"Good morning, Bill." Eli turned in his chair to face his employer and mentor. "What can I do for you?"

"I need you, Eli."

Eli's brows rose. "For?"

"I need you to go back down to Cypress Corners."

Cypress Corners, located in Central Florida, was one of Chapman's most successful projects. He'd been impressed during his short visit there back in the spring. A sprawling property of ten thousand acres featuring upscale retail, state-of-the-art homes and an award-winning golf course, it was also the home of Bill's children. The guy had three sons and a daughter who all fled to Florida and never came back.

Eli sat back, taking in the man's appearance from head to toe. Bill was tall and broad and still hearty at his age. He shared his thick, dark hair and his build with his sons. When Eli had met the eldest, Rick, he'd seen the stamp of a Chapman on his face. The guy's brothers might be a bit more laid back than the Sales Director of Cypress Corners, but Rick had been as cordial to Eli as Jake and Ben Chapman had been when he'd visited. They'd never let him get too close, though. The tours he'd taken with Rick's sales staff had been decidedly Chapman-free.

"I know Rick was a little prickly when you and Derek were down there in April," Bill said, settling into the chair across from him.

True, Rick had seemed a little suspicious of Eli's motives for coming to the development, but the tale wasn't his to tell.

Eli brushed off his comment with a smile. "He was very accommodating."

The statement was true. Rick had generously arranged the different tours he and Derek took—the sales pitch, the eco-tours, the new construction. And while legal eagle Derek had been busy calculating the risks and liabilities of what Chapman was planning down in Central Florida, Eli chose to focus on the scenery.

The place was a contradiction. That was for sure. Cypress Corners differed from most pricey developments Eli had visited. Championship golf course, boutiques and shops and custom homes were bracketed by conservation areas set aside for native plants and wildlife. Seventy percent was set aside, to be exact. It was different, but Eli had been drawn to the wild parts of Cypress as much as the civilized parts of the village. Not to mention the hot women that seemed to populate the place. *Damn.*

"Still," Bill went on. "I need you to get down there right away. Development is underway on the east side of the property, the planning anyway. I want Chapman to get a foothold there before another investor can even think of muscling in."

"Muscling in?" Eli quirked a smile at him. "What, are we going to the mattresses?"

Bill barked out a laugh. "Yes, I suppose I do sound like something from an old gangster movie."

Eli nodded. "Yeah, see," he said out the side of his mouth in a bad New York accent.

Bill smiled, losing some of the rigidity that always clung to him. This was Eli's gift, saying or doing whatever it took to get the job done. He was a terminal people-pleaser, but he preferred to think of himself as a survivor.

"Is this the Active Adult development?" he asked.

"Among other things."

"Such as?"

"There will be retail out that way as well," Bill said. "Upscale and plentiful, to satisfy folks happily spending their children's inheritance."

Eli mentally shrugged off the absent pang he felt at Bill's words. He had no one to leave him a damn thing, let alone spend it before he could get his hands on it.

He leaned forward. "What do you want me to do, exactly?"

"Get down there and get in at the Sales Center. I know Rick would like to see you come on board."

Eli doubted that. "Really." It wasn't a question.

"Yes. When I was down there for Raffaella's christening last month, I mentioned it to him."

"I bet that went over big with Ben and Tammy. Talking business at their celebration."

Bill waved a hand. "They're so over the moon for that adorable little ravioli they barely noticed."

The little ravioli. Bill's new granddaughter. That made two grandchildren for Bill, and Eli knew another one was on the way. The guy didn't see the family he had very often. Eli didn't know what had gone down between Bill and his kids, but Eli wouldn't break the tenuous connection he had here to risk the fallout if he started asking personal questions.

"How long do you need me to be down there?"

"Let's leave it open-ended, Eli. I trust you can handle anything that might come up here or at our other properties from Cypress?"

"Of course," Eli said. "Is Derek coming with me this

time?"

Bill shook his head. "No. I need him for some contract work up here in Boston."

Eli was almost relieved that Derek wouldn't come along. The guy was a little intense, and Eli had gotten tired of playing sweetness and light to offset his gloom and doom. Real fast.

"When do I leave?"

Bill's blue eyes lit up. "I knew I could count on you."

Relief nearly swamped him as he ate up the simply-worded praise. He flashed a bright smile.

"Always."

That settled, they discussed the details of Eli's upcoming return to Cypress Corners.

***

Cypress Corners, Florida

"Caroline! Time for dinner!"

Caroline Richmond shifted on the couch, holding the nubby green accent pillow over her face. Her mother's voice funneled up the steep staircase to rattle Caro's front door. Why couldn't her mother remember that Caro wasn't a teenage girl but a woman of twenty-seven? She owned her own business, for God's sake.

Grumbling, she sat up and rubbed her hands over her face. A glance at her phone showed her it was nearly six o'clock. Waking up at the butt-crack of dawn to bake enough treats to fill the cases of her shop made her afternoon naps a necessary evil. Still, she often awoke disoriented. Her mother's insistent voice didn't help her wake gently today. That was for sure.

True, she did still live under her parents' roof. Technically, at least. On days like this, when her mother made her feel like she was fourteen? She clung to the technicality until her knuckles cracked.

Her apartment above the oversized, three-car garage was a one-bedroom. It featured a kitchen trimmed with light granite and scaled-down stainless steel appliances. The living room shared the space with the kitchen, leaving her just enough room for her comfy couch and a TV. It was comfortable and pretty spacious for what it was, and the slanted ceilings gave it character.

If she kept the plantation shutters closed on the windows that overlooked her parents' impeccably-landscaped back yard and pool, she could almost imagine she lived there completely autonomously. That the gorgeous view of the main lakeshore across the street was hers alone.

"Caroline!"

She rolled her eyes and stood. Apparently there would be no time for fantasies this evening. She shoved her feet into her Keds and grabbed her cell phone. "Coming!"

She winced. Jeez, she sounded like a fourteen-year-old now. She went into her pretty marble-lined bathroom off the living area and peered into the mirror. Her little nap had given her customary ponytail a decided slant. She pulled the ponytail holder out of her hair and ran a brush through her waves, taking a lusty yawn. A splash of cool water on her face and she was ready for whatever Suzy-Homemaker meal her mother was serving in the main house.

Dawn Richmond was on a hearty home-cookin' kick lately. Caro figured the woman watched way too much of that show where the woman lived on a ranch and cooked tons of food for her brood. Her mother had no brood left in the house but Caro, not that it seemed to matter. That thought caused the usual conflicting emotions of guilt and resentment to trickle through her.

She headed down the stairwell and outside to follow the short path toward the back of her parents' house. At least her place had its own entrance. Her sneakers didn't make a sound on the flagstone path and when she walked through the opened French doors to the kitchen she found her mother humming as she ladled vegetables over a hearty-looking pot roast. She might act like she was cooking for ranch hands but with her still-trim figure and neat country-club-casual clothes she looked more Hamptons than Midlands.

"Pot roast, Mom?" she asked, shutting the doors to leave the heat outside. "It's September. In Florida."

Her mother nodded as she added more carrots and potatoes to the serving dish. "Yes, Caroline. I'm aware of that." Her gaze flicked over her from head to toe. "Is that what you're wearing?"

Caro wore her usual, capris and a T-shirt. She'd changed her top when she'd gotten home from work, and tonight's shirt was in a vintage red and one of her favorites. "What's the right answer to that question, Mom?"

Her mother returned her attention to the big hunk of braised beef. Caro crossed to the stainless fridge, it looked like the big daddy of the one in her apartment, and grabbed a diet soda. "You've made a lot, too. Are we expecting someone?"

Her mother froze before giving her a small smile. "Why, yes we are!"

Dread curled in Caro's belly. "Who?"

"I invited the golf pro, Caroline. Your father just raves about him."

"And what about him, exactly?" As if Caro couldn't guess.

Her mother placed the now-empty pot in the deep sink and wiped her hand on a perfectly-pressed dish towel. Caro knew the woman was stalling. She took in another breath and slowly let it out. Thank God for yoga.

"What about him, Mom?"

"He's recently divorced, is all. The poor man finds himself adrift. He could use a nice, home-cooked meal."

The golf pro. Kent something-or-other. He came into the bakery now and again. Tall guy, with a roving eye and wandering hands, if her friend Becky was being truthful.

"He dated Becky last month," Caro said. "Just how recent was his divorce?"

Her mother's cheeks reddened and Caro had her answer. "He is on his own now, Caroline. That's all I know."

"I'll just bet."

Dawn narrowed her eyes on her. "Are you comparing me to Charlotte Fairfax, dear?"

Caro gave her a practiced shrug. "I'm just sayin'."

Her mother braced her hands on her hips. "I don't gossip."

"Lettie doesn't gossip, Mom. Not exactly, anyway."

Her mother's shoulders dropped a fraction. "Well, Lettie did tell me that his little fling with Becky from the Cypress Institute was over now."

"His little fling?" Caro snorted. "Yeah, it's over. Becky kicked him to the curb when she found out his divorce wasn't final yet."

Her mother didn't say anything to that. She just started to set the table in the dining nook. Apparently they would share a casual meal with Kent the slime ball. *Great.*

"Just grab the bread basket, would you?" her mother asked. "The sourdough should be heated through."

Caro bit her tongue as she helped her mother with what would surely be yet another set-up for their little failure-to-launch. Her two brothers and one sister, all much older than Caro, were married and settled throughout Central Florida. A law professor and two lawyers in their father's firm, her siblings were successful and very sweet to their little sister. Their parents' later-life surprise. At least *they* didn't meddle in her love life.

"I'm not interested in Kent, Mom."

"Why not?" her father boomed as he came in through the

door from the garage. "He's a guy with prospects, Caroline."

Caro faced her father, keeping her expression even. "Prospects, Dad?"

Her father shrugged off his suit jacket and loosened his tie, leaning in to give her mother's cheek and then hers a kiss. "He's in play, Caroline. In demand."

Caro rolled her eyes. "Yes, he's very skilled at showing bored housewives how to hit a little white ball into a hole."

"Caroline!" her mother scolded. "He'll be here soon. You will behave."

She was about to tell her mother just how she planned to behave in the presence of Kent and his prospects when her phone buzzed. Sliding it out of her pocket, she saw that Becky sent her a text.

Wings and a game of pool?

Caro grinned at the screen. Yeah, an uncomplicated Friday night dinner with her friend at the End Zone in St. Cloud was just the escape she needed. She texted back in the affirmative and furrowed her brows.

"Mom. Dad. I have to meet Becky tonight. She's really broken-up over Kent, and I don't feel right having dinner with him."

Her parents stared at her, identical expressions of doubt and dismay on their faces.

"Caroline, your mother planned this dinner for you."

"I know, Dad." Caro took in another cleansing breath before continuing. "I don't need this dinner. I don't need a set-up and I sure as heck don't need Kent."

They stood there, her mother looking a little sad now. Caro kissed them both on the cheek and smiled.

"I wish you wouldn't worry about me, Dad. The dinner smells delicious, Mom. I'm sure Kent will appreciate all of your hard work."

After a long pause, her father gave a firm nod. "Go, sweetheart."

She knew he indulged her, as her mother often did, but she took the escape his simple command gave her. There was no way she was running into Kent right now so she dashed out of the house the back way, got into her bright green mini Cooper, and headed to St. Cloud. The city was about ten minutes to the west of Cypress, and she used the time and distance to consider her narrow escape.

She wouldn't stay out late tonight. Four o'clock came early in the morning, after all. Even on a Saturday. But she would have wings and maybe a beer, and shoot a couple of games of pool as she put her parents' latest attempt to run her life out of her mind. She was running her own life, thank you very much. Or at least, most of it.

Now if she could just figure out how to run the rest of it.

The sports bar in St. Cloud was crowded, which wasn't a big surprise for a Friday night. She parked her car between a chrome-encrusted Harley and a pickup truck raised high enough that she could have parked her mini underneath it. She chose to ignore the pair of metal balls dangling off the rear of the truck as she grabbed her bag and clicked her remote to lock her car.

"Hey, there!" Becky grinned as she waved Caro over to where she sat at a high two-top table set not far from the digital jukebox.

Caro smiled and felt the tension from her recent interaction with her parents drop off of her shoulders.

"Hey, Becky." She stepped up and sat in the vacant chair. "Oh, I need this."

"Do I want to know?" Becky asked, sipping what looked like a mojito.

Caro gave a dramatic shiver and raised her hand to signal a server.

A perky woman with a swinging ponytail bounced over.

"Pumpkin ale, if you've got it," Caro told her.

"Yep!" the server chirped as she set a cocktail napkin on the table. "Bottle or tap?"

"Tap, thanks." She placed her bag over the back of her chair and sighed. "Maybe I should have ordered a bottle. Portion control."

"Oh, relax," Becky said. "I've never seen you drink more than one or two beers anyway."

"True." Caro blew out a breath. "My parents tried to set me up with Kent."

Becky's blue eyes went round. "That slime ball? Seriously?"

"No worries. I shut that down. Even if he was remotely my type, I'd never do that to you."

Becky tucked a thick strand of red hair behind one ear and shrugged. "It's not like I loved the jerk."

"Still." The server brought her glass and Caro held it aloft. "Girl code."

Becky smiled, and then glanced over her shoulder for a second. Pursing her lips, she deliberately stirred her drink. "And just what is your type?"

19

Caro sipped her beer. "Hmm?"

"Tall, gorgeous and blond?" Becky went on. "Maybe he was hanging around Cypress a few months ago, taking his dazzling smile and broad shoulders with him when he left without a trace? Is that guy your type?"

Caro's silly heart fluttered. *That guy.* The blond guy from Chapman who'd flirted and teased whenever she'd run into him at the coffee shop or around the town square. Elijah Graham. Eli. Yum.

"What was his name, Caro?" Becky mused aloud. "Elliot?"

Caro swallowed. "Eli."

Becky smacked her hand on the table. "That's it! And just look who's back in town."

Turning her head slightly, Caro saw it was him. And he was just as gorgeous as she remembered. His gaze met hers and the flutters in her heart settled in her belly. Yeah, this guy. This guy was definitely her type. He sure wasn't the answer to her problems. But at the moment?

She couldn't even remember what they were.

Chapter 2

Eli glanced around the interior of the End Zone. It was dim inside but the large dining room to the right was lined all around with TVs set high on the walls broadcasting fishing shows and Ultimate Fighting matches. The scent of French fries and buffalo wings hung in the air, making his mouth water. There were few families seated at the wooden tables and booths, he supposed that was to be expected on a Friday night after all, but plenty of couples and pairs of couples. The singles? Belly-up-to-the-bar, mostly. Maybe he should make his way over there, too.

The drive from Orlando International Airport had taken about half an hour, but that was after the ridiculously long lines at the rental car place. He and Derek had come to the sports bar a few times back in the spring, and as he'd faced the choice of a left turn toward Cypress Corners or a right turn toward the bar it had been an easy decision. He could check into the Cypress Inn later. It was almost seven, and he hadn't eaten anything since grabbing a sub at Logan Airport.

He'd left his jacket in the SUV he'd rented and now he reached up to loosen his tie. Smiling absently at the waitress with a ponytail who passed a little too close to him, he headed toward the long bar stretched along the back wall. The wait staff buzzed around with round trays of food and drink. Some country pop song was playing on the digital juke box and the crack of cue against ball could be heard through the wide opening toward the room to his left.

"Hey, there," ponytail said as she returned, tilting her head to one side. "What would you like?"

He brushed off the obvious double-entendre and settled on a stool. "Bottle of Bud."

She clearly wanted to stay planted in front of him but several calls of "miss" drew her back to her job.

"Be right back," she said as she hurried behind the bar.

His beer appeared before him less than a minute later and he lifted it to his lips as he turned on his stool. The place was crowded and loud, and he ran his gaze around the room. There was the usual collection of dude bros and rednecks, as well as guys dressed in business casual like he was, obviously looking to blow off some steam at the end of the work week. Eli could sympathize. He didn't get much chance to just chill back in Boston. Bill Chapman kept him on speed dial, and a short leash if Derek's dark opinions could be believed. As if on cue, his phone chirped in his pocket.

He drew it out with one hand and saw he had a text from

Bill.

Did you arrive okay?

A smile teased Eli's lips. Guys Bill's age tended to text in full sentences.

Yes. Okay.

Good. Text me Monday after work.

Check in, he clearly meant. Report on Cypress and his son Rick. Maybe even the rest of his children too.

Will do, Eli typed back.

There wasn't an answering text from that one, and Eli didn't expect one. Bill was concise. To the point. He said what he wanted and that was that.

Pocketing his phone, he caught a woman's laughter and lifted his head. There, over by the jukebox, sat two girls he remembered seeing in Cypress Corners. Two hot and pretty girls, actually. The redhead worked at the Institute, he thought. The hotter one, the one with honey-colored curls, worked in the bakery and sometimes the coffee shop. His nostrils flared. She always smelled like cupcakes, he recalled. Warm and sweet. Stepping down, he made his way over to their table.

The redhead saw him first, and her lips curved in a smile. The other girl must have caught her friend's reaction because she turned her head. His breath caught. Damn, she was prettier than he remembered. Her face was heart-shaped, her lips plump. Her eyes looked green tonight, but he'd thought they were blue.

"Hi," he said. *Brilliant starter.*

"Hi, there," the redhead said, straightening in her seat. "Eli, is it?"

"Eli Graham." He nodded. "And you're…"

"Becky." She stuck out her hand and he shook it. "Becky Rollins. I work at the Cypress Institute."

He nodded to her, but his gaze was drawn to her friend again. That girl flipped some of her curls over her shoulder as she turned to face him and he caught that familiar scent of vanilla.

"Hi," she said.

Whoa. Her voice was sweet and a little husky. His belly tightened a little.

"You're Caroline Richmond right?" he asked.

Her brows rose. "Yes. Caro, actually. To everyone but my family."

He didn't know why he'd remembered her name, but her nickname seemed to fit her better. It was on the short side, like her. She probably wasn't taller than five foot four inches. And spunky. Also like her, unless he missed his guess.

"Caro," he repeated.

He watched her chest rise as she took in a breath. Her breasts were round and full beneath a soft-looking T-shirt that was worn in all the right places.

"Yes," she said again.

The redhead, Becky, snorted as she finished her drink. "Do you shoot pool, Eli?"

He nodded. "I can handle a stick."

"The tables are all taken," Caro rushed out.

He couldn't argue with that. From his vantage point he could see people standing around waiting for tables to open up. Still, it bothered him that she was giving him the brush-off.

"Another time?" he asked her.

She licked her lips as she lifted her glass of beer. "Maybe."

Now that, he liked to hear. He was always the guy who could turn a maybe into a yes. It was how he made his living, after all.

Ponytail came back with a big plate of wings, which she set on the table between the two women. She shot him a look of interest. "Are you joining them?"

He watched Caro bristle and Becky grin, and made a

decision. "That might be fun."

Ponytail dragged a chair over to him, brushing really close again as she set a stack of three small plates and some napkins down on the table's scarred surface. "It's a tight squeeze."

He glanced down her low-cut shirt and silently agreed. She left them and Eli faced Caro. "May I?"

Leaning her arms on the table, she shrugged. "Sure."

He wedged himself closer to her side of the table and watched as Becky tried without success to hide her smile.

"So what are you two ladies up to tonight?" he asked.

"Drowning our sorrows," Becky said.

"That seems pretty dark for a Friday night," he said.

"It's nothing that serious." Caro fingered the condensation on the side of her glass, and he watched her slender fingers for a long minute. "I had to escape a family dinner tonight."

"A family dinner featuring a fix-up with my ex," Becky added as she served herself some wings.

Eli might have envied the family part of this conversation, but not the fix-up. He dug into the wings himself. "Seriously?"

Caro took a couple of wings to place them neatly on her plate. "My mother had heard some great things about the guy."

"Lies!" Becky laughed. "The guy is a slug, which my good

friend here knew already."

"What did slug man think about your escape?" he asked.

"I didn't hang around to find out." Caro wiped her fingers on a napkin. "I can't believe they tried that."

"I can't believe you need a fix-up," he said.

Both women gaped at him and he realized what he'd said. Becky crossed her arms and leaned back as Caro continued to just look at him. What was she thinking?

The server came back. "Are you doing okay?"

"Let me get the next round," he said.

"No more for me," Caro said.

"Aw, come on," Becky said. "It's early."

"I have to get up at four tomorrow morning, Becky."

"Why?" Eli asked.

She leveled a look at him. "So you remember my name but not what I do?"

He blinked at her, and then snapped his fingers when it hit him. "The bakery."

"Got it in one try," Becky said.

He knew when a strategic retreat was necessary. Caro was giving off a serious leave-me-alone vibe. This wasn't the time to turn on his charm to try to get the pretty blond in his bed at the inn.

"I'll let you two talk, then. Thanks for letting me crash." He grabbed his beer bottle and stood, and then put a twenty on the table. "I guess I'll see you around Cypress."

"You will?" Caro's cheeks turned pink.

"I sure will. I'm going to be working there now."

***

Caro stared at the man standing very close to her. Perched as she was on the tall chair, she didn't have to tip her head too far back to meet his pretty blue gaze.

"You're going to be working at Cypress?"

"Yep. At the Sales Center."

"Cool," Becky put in. "You'll be working with some great people."

"I'm looking forward to it." He held his bottle up with a nod. "Have a good night."

When he started to walk away, she couldn't help but watch. He looked truly fine in his expensive clothes. Wide shoulders and a sculpted butt, not to mention long strong legs. He really was going to give her and Becky their space tonight. Then he turned to face her again, and the view improved exponentially. Oh, he looked yummy.

"I'll see you in the morning, Caro," he said.

"What?" She gaped at him for the second time tonight. "Why?"

He shrugged and flashed the sexiest smile she'd ever seen. "For a cupcake."

He turned away again and Becky snickered.

Caro shot her a look. "Don't start."

"He likes you," Becky sang softly.

"Stop that," Caro whispered.

The server came back, eyeing Eli's vacant chair with a smirk before looking at her and Becky. "Another round?"

Caro shook her head but Becky nodded.

"Just for me, thanks," Becky said. "My friend here has to make cupcakes in the morning."

Caro chuckled as the server left to get Becky's drink. "What was that, exactly?"

"Hey, Eli has a sweet tooth." She winked as she rattled the ice in her glass. "And I'll bet it's not just cupcakes he wants."

Caro chose to ignore that little tidbit.

Her alarm buzzed her awake at four o'clock on the dot. She'd gotten home from the End Zone right around ten, which was early as far as Friday nights out went. It was par for the course where she was concerned, however. She laughed to herself at that thought. Kent the slime ball would have liked that one.

"Ick," she grumbled as she quickly showered and got dressed for work.

Darkness still pressed against her windows, but she'd grown used to that. There was only so much prep that could be done the afternoon before, especially when you wanted to offer fresh-baked treats to the visitors and residents of Cypress. Dressed in her usual work attire, another pair of capris topped by a spring green T-shirt emblazoned with the bakery's name, Sweet Escape, in pink and white scrolled letters, she pulled her hair back into a ponytail, tied her Keds and headed downstairs.

The morning was humid and dark, and the security light snapped on the second she stepped out onto the drive. Dew blanketed her car, so when she started it she ran the wipers a couple of times before heading out to the bakery.

Sweet Escape, her own tiny slice of independence, sat in a prime location next to the coffee shop in the town square. It had picture windows on either side of its front door, and was just a couple of storefronts in from the corner. This made it convenient to both the Sales Center and the restaurants across the street. For nearly two years now she'd been in business, and everyone at Cypress had been very welcoming. It didn't hurt that she was supplying their ever-growing demand for sweets both decadent and, more and more often, vegan or gluten-free.

She parked in the space reserved for Sweet Escape employees at the back of the row of shops, right next to where Jane's bicycle was chained to the sign declaring it so. Jane, her invaluable baking assistant, had beaten her in. Again.

Caro opened the back door to find the alarm shut off and the overhead lights flickering on. Locking the door behind her, she walked into the kitchen to find Jane humming to herself as she began to prep for their day.

"Good morning, Jane."

Jane, a trim woman of about fifty years, waved a hand and straightened. "Good morning, boss."

"You know, you don't have to get here when I do."

"I don't." Jane winked. "I get here before you do."

Caro smiled. "Never mind."

Jane went about her very-efficient business, her humming soon mingling with the sounds of mixers whirring and the ovens clicking on and off as they maintained the optimum baking temperatures for the incoming sweets. The woman was dressed as Caro was, trading sneakers for the crocs she kept at the back door. As Jane stirred bowls and filled cupcake tins, Caro woke up the computer in the tiny back room that served as an office and supply closet and double-checked the orders that would go out to their distributors.

Cardboard and string and tape and stickers shared the space with her computer. Several refrigerators in the kitchen held their most important supplies though, along with ventilated metal shelves to hold dry goods and decorations.

It was all matter-of-fact to her now, but in the beginning Caro had a tough time getting the hang of things. She'd never run a business and, despite her degree in hospitality management from the University of Central Florida, she'd had to find her own way to make this particular little business work. Luckily she'd yet to meet a person here, living in or visiting Cypress, that didn't have at least a little bit of a sweet tooth.

The thought made her think about Eli. Would he really come by this morning, or was he just trying to get laid? She'd been around a couple of times, after all. She knew she possessed certain physical attributes attractive to the superficial male. She'd bought into a guy's pick-up line a few times, too. Her slime-ball radar was pretty good now, though. Hadn't she known

32

Kent for a slug right away? Eli didn't set her radar off, but that could be because he was quite possibly the hottest guy she'd ever seen. Even his voice was delicious.

"Cupcakes in the oven," Jane said, poking her head into back room. "I'll go ahead and start on the s'mores brownies. Are you making them the special today?"

Caro thought for a second. The brownies were a Sweet Escape specialty, done with marshmallow creamed swirled throughout and sprinkled liberally with graham cracker crumbs. Their secret was a wave of the torch to the uppermost marshmallows to give them a real campfire s'mores taste.

"Sure." She wondered if Eli would like them. "Make plenty. With the afternoons at least a little bit cooler now, we might be busy up until closing."

Jane gave her usual firm nod and took herself back into the kitchen. The bakery was open from seven in the morning until three in the afternoon, and Sunday was their day of rest. It had nothing to do with religion, but her father had told her that you had to build in free time to breathe when you ran your own business. He should know. Richmond and Richmond (and let's face it, Richmond) was a very successful law firm yet he and both Robbie and Sherry managed to have family lives outside of the firm. Her youngest brother Phillip, ten years older than she, often bragged that as a professor he got the whole summer off. She hadn't seen much of him or her other siblings this summer, though. The holidays would bring them all home to roost, and wouldn't Phillip tease her about how she still lived at home.

Putting the overachieving Richmond children out of her mind, she joined Jane in the kitchen and tied on one of the full aprons hanging on hooks fresh and ready for the new day. She set on the task of putting the finishing touches on a little boy's seventh birthday cake. It was to be decorated for a party at the main lakeshore, so she'd already frosted it a blue-gray like the water of the lake and had the trees to fill in this morning.

"Blue-gray?" Jane clicked her tongue. "I never would have thought of it, but it is pretty."

"It's the lake, Jane." Caro turned the cake board to show her. "See? I'll add more rippling waves for depth."

"Don't forget the alligator."

Caro laughed. "I wouldn't think of it! Cypress might have its own Wildlife Tech on staff to make sure no real ones wander into the little guy's party, but they still love the sweet ones."

"You make their faces so cute," Jane said. "All of the animals you make. They're friendly-looking but also realistic. At least, I assume so. I'll take your word on that, thanks."

"Not *my* word. I'm so not an outdoors kind of girl."

"You and me both."

"You ride your bike to and from work, Jane."

"And I ride pretty fast, too."

The oven dinged, and Jane went back to work. Caro did as well, adding details like trees and moss, and creating a gator resting across one corner of the large sheet cake. She was humming now too, and lost herself in the scent of sweet icing and the art of working with it. It was moments like this that she felt the most grateful for this chance to make her dream come true.

This part of her life? Her Sweet Escape? This was going just great.

Chapter 3

Eli stepped out of the nicely-appointed bathroom on
Saturday morning in his room at the Cypress Inn, rubbing one of
the thick towels over his wet head. He draped the towel over the
chair beside the small desk and pulled on his boxer briefs and a
pair of cargo shorts. It was still pretty early, especially for a
Saturday morning, but he was never one to hang around in bed
even if he was alone. He never had that luxury as a kid and, even
if he did now, he was accustomed to rising soon after the sun.

He'd stayed in the inn, a bed and breakfast really, last
spring, and despite the inn's being quaint and full of what he
guessed was Southern charm in the lobby and the common areas,
the guest rooms were modern and comfortable and filled with
the style and amenities people would expect at any of
Chapman's properties. He should know. He'd stayed in enough
of them over his three years working at Chapman Financial. Bill
hadn't been able to get his hands on this little slice of Cypress.
Not yet, anyway.

Three stories tall, the B and B sat on a rise not far from the
main lakeshore. It was designed well, and situated in a near-
perfect setting. A huge wraparound porch and wide balconies off
of several of the fifteen guest rooms took advantage of the view.

He pulled on a pale green polo and stepped into his sneakers, and then crossed to his balcony.

The sun was already up, and the air was humid and getting warmer. When he'd been here in the spring the heat had been welcome after the long winter of cold, wet weather in Boston. Now, though? He longed for the crisp fall air where he'd grown up.

A memory tickled at the back of his mind, one of being bundled up against the chill and gathering crisp colorful leaves with a nameless, faceless woman he could only assume was his mother. She might have been one of his early foster mothers, though. Or maybe an older girl in the group home he'd landed in several times between more permanent, temporary placement. Even though he'd aged out of the foster system over ten years ago, he still felt like that lost little boy sometimes. He was nearly thirty, for God's sake.

He caught the frown on his face in the glass of the French door. Clearing his expression, he pulled the door open and stepped outside. The view of the lakeshore was as beautiful as he remembered, and he settled into one of the wicker chairs on the balcony. He stretched his long legs out toward the filigreed wrought-iron railing and let out a breath.

He'd had a text from Rick Chapman last night, which he'd read when he'd gotten back from the End Zone, telling him to take the weekend to settle in and come to the Sales Center on Monday morning. Eli had received and signed the docs accepting the offer of employment before he'd left Boston, so he was all set to start work at Cypress Corners. It wasn't where he'd imagined being this autumn, but he went wherever Bill needed him. Besides that, he'd told Caro he'd see her in Cypress.

Caro. The girl was something. Her parents had tried to fix her up? Why? She was gorgeous. Any guy with eyes in his head could see that. She was smart too, seeing that she ran her own business. She was a catch, not that he was baiting the hook or anything. Whenever he caught a girl, he wasted little time cutting her loose once the good times were over. And they were generally over pretty quick.

A few of them seemed to want more from him. Hell, a couple had outright told him as much. He was better on his own, charming his way through work and women and keeping everything light and easy.

Eli knew he was good at his job, and traveling to far-flung properties on Chapman's behalf was part and parcel of his position. He'd traveled more than he'd ever dreamed of back when he'd been a kid. Hell, he had more money now that he'd ever dreamed of, too. He had yet to figure out how to do the rest of it, though. Friends and hanging out and just being himself. That emotional stuff was never a good fit for him. In his experience, tears were brushed off and anger dismissed in his foster homes, and he'd learned to hide everything behind a look alternating between calm and good humor. He wasn't even sure what he was hiding anymore.

The inn had claim to a private beach reserved for its guests. Soft sand, gentle waves and towering trees dripping with Spanish moss all added to the feeling of seclusion. The beach was empty at the moment, though. It was quiet from the beach to the east of the inn, too. That was the main lakeshore, he knew from his previous visit. It was one of the many attractions geared toward for families that Cypress touted in all of their tours and literature.

He supposed he should get up-to-speed on all of the amenities and quick. If he expected to sell Cypress? He had to buy into it himself. Maybe a walk around the town square on a sunny Saturday morning would help him get his bearings.

A smile teased his lips. The bakery would be open this morning. The lovely Caroline had said as much last night, hadn't she? He wasn't sure why he'd flirted with her, other than the obvious. Yes, she was hot. And when she blushed her eyes seemed to change color. But she had a lot of family looking after her. That was clear to him. He had no clue how to deal with family, and if he got involved with her even a little bit, there would be complications.

When he went downstairs to the bottom floor of the inn, he found breakfast set in the dining room. There were pastries on trays and several kinds of fruit for guests to serve themselves. The coffee smelled delicious and drew him further into the room. There weren't many guests present, and he figured that it was a little too early for them.

The French doors were open to the large balcony beyond, and he poured some coffee into a paper cup and strolled outside. The view of the lake met his gaze again.

"Didn't you want to try one of our cinnamon rolls, Mr. Graham?"

Eli smiled at the innkeeper, an older woman of compact proportions. "I don't think so, Mrs. Rollins."

"They're an exclusive," the woman added with a grin. "Not even the bakery in town has them."

"I'm sure they're delicious, but I'll have to try one

tomorrow."

She placed her hands on her ample hips and tilted her graying head to the side. Her hair held a lot of red in it, and he absently wondered if she was related to Caro's friend, Becky Rollins.

"You're not working on a Saturday, are you?" she asked.

"No," he said. "Not this Saturday, anyway."

"You're going to work at the Sales Center, right?"

Eli nodded, causing the woman's smile to widen.

"There you go! No one works at the Sales Center on the weekends."

Eli stilled. This was news to him. "What?"

"Yes, sir," she went on. "Mr. Forbes, and that lovely Rick Chapman, insist that the place close on the weekends so that folks can spend time with family."

Family. There was that word again.

"That's, um. Different. I didn't know that."

"I guess you're used to working through your weekends up in Boston?"

He arched a brow and she laughed lightly.

"It's impossible to keep secrets in Cypress Corners, Mr. Graham."

He flashed her his trademark smile and her eyelashes fluttered.

"Then it's a very good thing I'm an open book, Mrs. Rollins."

She giggled, actually giggled, and Eli dipped his head and stepped around her out into the lobby. His mind worked around what the woman had said. What the hell? The Sales Center was closed on the weekends? He thought back to when he and Derek had been here in the spring, and realized that the tours and conversations he'd had with Rick Chapman and any of his people had been on weekdays.

"Real observant, dumb ass," he grumbled.

The dew of the morning was burning off, if the rising temperature was any indication. It would be warm today, but he had hopes that it wouldn't be oppressive. He might not have any plans for his first of what would apparently be many Saturdays off, but he still wanted to explore Cypress and get a real feel for the place.

He took another sip of his coffee and got into his SUV parked on the crushed shell lot behind the inn. His stomach growled and he regretted passing on one of Mrs. Rollins's exclusive cinnamon buns. An idea struck him, and it was almost stupid it was so obvious. Setting the cup in the holder, he pulled out of the lot and headed toward the town center. If he was going to get a feel for the place, where better to start than with the bakery?

And if he wanted to flirt with the sweet little baker? That sure seemed like a great way to pass his first day off in months.

***

It was nearly seven o'clock, and Sweet Escape was just about ready to open.

"The kid's here," Jane said as she grabbed the tray of brownies. "She's doing a sweep of the dining area and making sure everything in the case looks great."

The kid Jane was talking about was Ashlyn, the college student Caro had hired to work on Saturdays and a couple of afternoons during the week. She was very good at her job, which was to make sure customers were greeted properly and the bake case looked crisp, clean and inviting. Caro could get a little bit OCD about the place, and thankfully both Ashlyn and Jane were as meticulous as she was.

Caro wiped her hands and put on a fresh apron, one of the short ones that let her shirt and logo show. A quick trip to the unisex bathroom showed her Ashlyn had been here too. It was clean and neat as a pin. Caro brushed the stray flour and a smudge of blue icing off of her face and attempted to smooth the curls trying to escape her ponytail. As she stepped out, Ashlyn was just unlocking the door. The girl opened it with a grin, as she did on mornings she was here, and the first five notes of the pop song Sweet Escape chimed.

"I love that," Ashlyn said. "It gets the song stuck in my head all day, though."

"You and me both," Jane put in.

Caro shook her head in mock severity. "Suck it up, buttercup."

Sweet Escape was open for business. The bakery had wide plank wood flooring and several wooden tables, some round and some square, painted or stained in difference finishes. An eclectic mix of chairs were set neatly at each. The walls were painted a lighter green than their shirts and bakery boxes, and the color was bright and soothing at the same time. A narrow shelf ringed the place, painted a creamy white to match the wainscoting beneath. Mason jars holding lifelike silk wildflowers in pinks and yellows and purples sat on the shelf, adding to the homey and welcoming feel. The scent of lemon oil lingered just beneath the combined sugary smells of Sweet

Escape's offerings.

Pride filled Caro every morning in this bit of time before the first customer entered and set off that pop-song chime, and this morning was no different. Pride that she'd done this without her family's help and pride that the business continued to pay for itself, after a rocky first year.

Her gaze settled on the wide display cases, in which the usual treats and their signature creations sat on glass plates over crisp doilies with tiny cards listing today's temptations. Ashlyn disappeared into the back to help Jane with a few more trays of treats as the familiar door chime rang behind her. She turned to face their first customer of the day.

"Welcome to Sweet Escape." She stilled, and gaped at Eli. "Oh, it's you."

"Good morning." He flashed that powerful smile of his and she felt the polished wood floor tilt just a little bit. "A sweet escape, huh?"

She couldn't help but smile. "I like to think so."

He ran a hand over his blond waves, and the action pulled up the bottom of his light green polo just a bit. She caught a glimpse of the lighter skin right above the low waistband of his shorts. Dragging her eyes from the sliver of skin more tempting than anything in the bake cases, she faced him again. By the sparkle in his blue eyes she guessed he'd seen where her attention had strayed.

"You're up early," she managed to say.

"It's the norm for me." He stepped closer and she caught the scent of him. It was fresh and a little spicy. "I'll have you know I turned down Mrs. Rollins's exclusive cinnamon rolls this morning."

Caro wrinkled her nose. "Oh, those darn cinnamon rolls. She's Becky's mother, you know. Those rolls are her only claim to make, and she lords them over me."

"Can't you make cinnamon rolls?"

"I can bake circles around the Cypress Inn, Eli."

He studied the treats arrayed in the display cases. "And yet, I don't see any."

She snorted. "And you won't. I think I have enough treats to put cinnamon rolls out of your mind."

His gaze flicked back to her, and ran slowly over the front of her. Her body tightened and her breasts tingled.

"Yeah, you do," he said.

The words were so brash, so clichéd, she couldn't help but laugh. "Well, you're still welcome." She walked around one of the bake cases to put the counter between them. "Would you like to try the special?"

When he wriggled his eyebrows she laughed again. "Don't even go there."

He laughed and tilted his head to look into the bake cases again. "Those brownies look amazing."

"Our s'mores brownies, Mr. Graham." She chuckled and he looked up at her in question. "Graham cracker."

He blinked, and then nodded. "I get it." He glanced at the case and then back at her. "Cupcake."

"So you want a cupcake?"

A smile curved his well-formed mouth. "Not touching that one. I'll try one of those s'mores brownies, though."

She nodded to Ashlyn, who bagged up one of the thick brownies while Caro rang him up. "Coffee this morning, too?"

"Is it plain coffee?"

"I can manage a latte if you prefer, but you have to go to the coffee shop for anything fancier."

"Plain coffee, please. Cream no sugar."

She poured him a coffee, leaving room for the cream she then added. Capping a plastic lid on the cup, she handed it and the bag to him.

He swiped his card to pay. "So what is there to do in Cypress on a Saturday?"

She shrugged. "Hmm. Let's see. There isn't anything this weekend. You just missed the Labor Day Picnic, but we'll have the Fall Festival in a couple of weeks. And then there's Halloween, which is celebrated longer than one day here. Cypress Corners is the small town afraid to be bored."

"I get that. I was here right before Easter." He took the lid off his coffee and blew into the cup a little. "They were just gearing up for what I guessed was an epic egg hunt."

"It was. Sorry you missed it?"

"Maybe." He unwrapped his brownie. "I do have a sweet tooth."

His eyes were on hers as he took a bite, but even he couldn't keep up his double entendre as the brownie's special mix of moist chocolate cake, chips and toasted marshmallow apparently melted on his tongue. He closed his eyes and moaned, making her have some very naughty thoughts.

"My God," he mumbled, wiping a napkin over his mouth. "I have to sit down. Thanks, Caro."

She laughed as he took his breakfast over to one of the tables near the window, making room for the customer who quickly stepped up to the counter.

She was soon too busy to pay him any more attention, and they had a line nearly to the door. Chatter and laughter mingled with the five-note door chime, and Jane and Ashlyn both pitched in. By the time the line thinned a little and she had a chance to look up, he was gone. It was nearly nine o'clock, after all. Still she was surprised to find she was disappointed, and wasn't that just silly?

He'd been flirting with her, but that seemed to be his default setting. Those sparkling eyes, that teasing mouth. That dusting of golden stubble over his strong jaw. Not to mention how good he looked in his casual clothes. He was built for flirting, and lots of other wicked stuff.

"Why don't you take a few minutes, boss lady," Ashlyn said in her ear. "Grab your morning cup of coffee."

"Hmm?" Caro stared at the girl for a beat. "What?"

"Jane and I have this." Ashlyn shouldered her way behind the counter. "Right, Jane?"

Jane called out her agreement as she set another plate of brownies in the case, and Caro took off her apron and poured herself a cup of coffee. A little bit of sugar and a lot of milk finished hers, and she took it outside. She smiled at the customers coming and going as she settled on one of the benches lining the sidewalk. Her cup of coffee might not be what the flock of people going in and out of the coffee shop were craving, but it was hot and strong and just what she needed at the moment. Taking a long sip, she closed her eyes and leaned back. She let out a little purr as caffeine soaked into her veins.

"I could watch you drink that all day."

Eli's voice stroked over her and she found herself smiling even before she opened her eyes. "Eli."

He sat down next to her, bracing his legs apart as he settled back himself. "Looks like you're having a busy morning."

"Thank God."

"This is *your* business, isn't it? Yours alone?"

She couldn't help but smile. "Yep. All mine."

He gave a nod of approval. "Good for you." He glanced at the door of the bakery as it opened and shut, and then arched a brow at her.

"What?" she asked. "Or do I even want to know?"

"Your bakery is closed on Sundays."

A tingle of anticipation went through her, and she tried her hardest to ignore it. "Yep. It is."

"Then we'll have to figure out how to fill our day off."

"*Our* day off?"

"Yeah, I'm not used to having a day off. Let alone two in a row. Tell me we can do something tomorrow?"

"What kind of something?"

"Is that a yes?"

She bit her lip, and then shrugged. "Sure. Why not?"

He leaned a little closer as he reached into his pocket for his phone. "Give me your number?" She did, and he typed it in. "I'll call you tomorrow, Cupcake."

"Cupcake?"

He leaned closer still, and she thought for a heart-stopping second that he was going to kiss her. Instead he seemed to breathe her in. "Yeah. The name suits you." He stood, shoving his hands in his pockets again and giving her another glimpse of that sweet sliver of pale skin well below his navel. "See you tomorrow."

"See you." She winked up at him. "Graham Cracker."

He barked out a laugh and took easy strides down the sidewalk toward the other shops.

She couldn't help but smile as she finished her coffee. She had a date, or something, with Eli Graham. The hottest guy she'd ever seen, and he seemed so easygoing. That was a good thing.

She'd done the emotional thing before and she was so not going there again.

Chapter 4

Eli sat at the bar in the town tavern, sipping a beer and waiting on the burger he'd ordered. He really had no clue what to do tonight. He'd spent his day off doing pretty much nothing at all, and that didn't feel right. He'd worked on his laptop in his room, answering some emails and seeing to some Chapman business, but even those tasks hadn't taken him very long. Not long enough, anyway.

"Hey, there," a guy said to his right. "Eli, right?"

Eli turned to find the blond builder, Noah something, walking toward him. He was dressed like Eli was, in a polo and shorts.

"Eli Graham, yes." They shook hands. "We met last spring."

"Noah Brady." His eyes narrowed. "You and that other Chapman guy were here back in April."

"Derek."

"Derek, yeah. You two put Jessie through her paces."

"Jessie?"

Noah raised his brows. "My wife. She toured the two of you when you were here."

Eli remembered the pretty little blonde then, but he

wouldn't admit that right now. This guy was as tall and as broad as he was, and he probably wouldn't like to know that Eli had enjoyed flirting with the little Pixie. Just flirting. Even if he'd wanted to close the deal, he had sensed something between the builder and Jessie on his last tour with them. He could read people pretty well. He'd had to learn how very early in life. Besides, if she was now his wife, Eli hadn't been too far off the mark.

"Yes, she really knows Cypress," Eli said. "She's still at the Sales Center, right?"

"She is. And you're starting there."

"On Monday."

Noah leaned an elbow on the bar. "I'm sure Rick Chapman and Mr. Forbes are happy to have you, with Tammy out."

"I'm eager to start and learn the ropes."

A male server brought a bag of food to the bar and Noah took it. He turned back to Eli. "I better get back. I was sent out to hunt up dinner, and they'll be hungry."

"Enjoy your dinner."

"Thanks," Noah said. "I'll see you on Monday."

"You will?"

"I work there too, Eli. When I'm not out on the job site."

Just like that, Eli got the message. He was warned off, but he could have told the guy he didn't have to. Jessie was off the market, and he never poached on another guy's woman.

"Then I guess I'll see you on Monday," Eli said.

Noah seemed to lose a little bit of the stick up his ass, and he even managed to smile before leaving the tavern.

Eli took a long drink of his beer. Yeah, he'd noticed Jessie when he'd been here. There were a lot of other pretty women here too, and for a second he wondered just what was in the water of the pristine lakes located throughout the property. Not one of the women had stuck in his head like Caro had, though.

She was gorgeous, but there was something else there too. Maybe he shouldn't get any closer to her. She didn't seem like a girl up for a fling, and he couldn't exactly indulge himself with someone he'd run into while he was here. And Bill Chapman wanted him here. To stay, or at least for the foreseeable future. Eli was surprised he'd arranged to put him up in the inn and not one of the rental houses available.

The bartender set his plate in front of him. "Can I get you anything else right now?" she asked.

Eli shook his head at her. "No, thanks."

She stepped further down the line, and Eli belatedly

noticed that the place was nearly full now. While he'd been having a pissing contest with Noah Brady, the tavern had gotten busy. It was located right next to the Clubhouse, the upper crust restaurant that was the showplace of Cypress. The Clubhouse was more Bill Chapman's speed than Eli's, although he'd eaten there on his last visit. He remembered there were lots of pressed linen and clinking crystal, and an air of superiority that always tended to give him the chills whenever he ate with Bill at places like that in Boston.

He pushed the thought aside and dug into his juicy, bloody burger. Wiping his mouth, he swallowed and thought about the coming day. For the first time in so long he couldn't remember, he had two free days in a row. He'd asked a woman to spend some time with him, too. A date, although he had a feeling that if he'd framed it like that she would have turned him down. That would have made things very uncomfortable when he went into the bakery. That was for sure.

He hadn't been lying when he said he had a sweet tooth. The double entendre had been fun, though. *She* seemed like she could be a lot fun, but he also thought she didn't let herself go very often.

"Do you want another beer?" The bartender was back.

"Sure." She nodded but before she could run away again he called her back. "Hey, what's fun to do around here?"

She slanted him a look. "Is that a line?"

He flashed a smile but shook his head. "Not at the moment, no. I have a date tomorrow and I want to take her someplace…easy."

"Easy?" Her brows knit. "Easy. I'd avoid the theme parks, then."

"Yeah, I don't feel like heading out to see the mouse," he said, referring to Disney World.

"What do you feel like doing?" she asked. "You could drive out to the beach."

"No, I don't think so." Not that he didn't like the idea of seeing what Caro looked like in a bikini. "And going to the movies wouldn't be good, either."

She thought a little more. "You could head to Old Town Village."

"What's that?"

"It's over in Kissimmee. Rides and games, and shops and restaurants too."

He thought for a second. It would be fun, and he guessed Caro could use some fun. "Yeah, maybe. How do I get there?"

"Just get on one-ninety-two and head west for about forty-five minutes until you come to the giant Ferris wheel on the left. You can't miss it."

"Great. Thanks."

She filled a mug with beer and set it in front of him. "She's a lucky girl."

"And thanks for that."

She wasn't flirting. Not really. And he wasn't flirting back. As she went down the bar once again, waiting on the customers seated there, he watched only absently. She was pretty, tall and dark-haired and maybe in her late twenties. He wasn't flattering himself when he thought that if he'd pursued he could probably get her in that plush bed in his room at the inn. He was known to close a deal when he wanted it badly enough. He didn't, though. Not tonight.

Tonight he'd think about walking around a place that had a Ferris wheel, of all things. Of seeing another one of Caro's beautiful smiles and maybe even messing around a little bit.

He might not be down for bedding the bartender but he couldn't help wondering if Caro tasted as sweet as she smelled.

***

"You're going out?"

58

Caro managed to keep from rolling her eyes as her mother asked her that question. The woman sounded almost shocked. It wasn't like Caro didn't date, after all. She just didn't usually let her mother know about it.

The woman had come up this morning with fresh bagels, the one thing she knew Caro couldn't resist since it wasn't something she made at Sweet Escape.

"Yes, Mom." She spread cream cheese on her everything bagel and took a bite, taking her time to chew and swallow before facing Dawn Richmond's inquisition again. "I'm going out."

"And where are you going?"

"I'm not sure."

In fact, Eli had been almost cryptic when he'd called her this morning. He'd just said they were going someplace fun, but she couldn't get anything more out of him.

Her mother poured them each a mug of coffee. "Who is he?"

"Why?"

Her mother blinked. "Why? Why wouldn't I want to know who my daughter is seeing?"

Caro drank her coffee, counting to ten before setting her

mug back down. "He's Eli Graham. He works here in Cypress."

"He works here? Well, who doesn't?"

"He's from Chapman Financial, if that means anything."

Her mother's eyes widened. "Ooh, Chapman Financial! That's promising."

"Promising?" Caro clicked her tongue. "Jeez, this isn't an Edwardian drama on PBS, Mom."

"I know." She laughed lightly. "I didn't mean to sound so stuffy."

"You're a lot of things, believe me. Stuffy isn't usually one of them."

Her eyes twinkled. "A lot of things?"

Caro considered telling her mother for the hundredth time that she didn't have to look after her. That she could live her own life, even though she lived that life above their garage. The woman wouldn't get it, though. Caro was her baby. Her surprise. And Caro also knew all of her meddling came from a place of love.

"Mom, I'm twenty-seven years old."

"I know that, dear."

"I own my own business."

"And your father and I are so proud of you."

"Yet you keep trying to fix me up with a man who can, I don't know, complete me somehow."

Her mother's face crumpled a little. "I worry about you, Caroline."

Caro closed her eyes. "I know."

She'd gotten engaged when she was twenty-three, and her parents had planned an elaborate wedding for their youngest child. Brad, a guy she'd known all through college, died in a car crash just two weeks before the ceremony, but he wasn't alone in the car. The girl he'd been sleeping with for months also died that night, and Caro had gone from grief to anger and back again for far too long. She'd totally missed that he was a slime ball, and that wasn't going to happen again.

When she looked at her mother again, she forced a bright smile. "This is just a date, Mom. It's not even really a date, I don't think."

"It's not a date! Who is this clown?"

Caro laughed. "Now he's a clown? I thought he was promising?"

Her mother laughed along with her. "Oh, I'm entitled to change midstream."

"Thanks for the bagels, but I should get ready." She stood.

"Not that I know what to wear. He said to dress for something fun and easy."

"Fun and easy?" Her mother looked as puzzled as Caro felt. "I'm intrigued."

"Good bye, Mom."

Her mother bustled around the kitchen, wiping the counter that was already clean. "Okay, okay." She carefully hung up the dish towel. "Have fun."

"That's the plan." She shrugged. "I think, anyway."

She was alone again, so she finished cleaning up and went into her bedroom to get dressed for her "fun and easy" day with Eli Graham.

Denim shorts, another vintage T-shirt in a shade of blue she couldn't help but think would match Eli's eyes, and sneakers then. She brushed her hair and left it down. It came just past her shoulders and if whatever it was he had planned was a little too much fun, she could pull it back into a ponytail. She grabbed her bag and unplugged her phone just as her doorbell rang. It couldn't be her mother, back again. She never rang the bell.

She glanced at her phone. Eleven on the dot. Just like he'd said. She turned to go, locking the door behind her and hurrying down the steep staircase. Opening the door at the bottom, she found Eli standing on the stoop. The peaked roof and concrete pad combined were a little too small for the stoop to be considered a porch, but the mat and small urns filled with pink geraniums at least kept it somewhat in scale with the giant coach lamp set to one side of the door. It matched the lights at the front of the house, and she knew how much her mother liked things to match.

"Hi, Eli." She stepped out and nearly bumped into him. He sure filled the space, and he smelled really good too. "You found the place okay?"

Her front door was set around the corner to the far right of the home's façade, and if you didn't know to look for it you'd probably miss it. He nodded, at last stepping back and giving her a little bit of breathing room. He wore shorts and a T-shirt too, appearing as casual as she was.

"Oh, good." She waved a hand over him. "You're dressed like me."

He grinned and then gazed up at the rest of the house. "Nice house."

"It's my parents'."

His brows arched and she held up a hand. "I live upstairs. Above the garage."

He nodded. "Big garage."

"Big apartment." She shouldered her bag. "Where to?"

"A place called Old Town Village. Have you been there?"

"Not in a while."

"The bartender at the tavern recommended it."

"It's fun." She smiled up at him. "And easy."

"Perfect." He winked. "Let's go, then."

He stepped behind her on the paved walk and followed her to the curb. An SUV was parked there, tall and broad like him. He opened the door for her and she climbed up and in.

"Nice."

"Rental," he answered.

He walked around and got behind the wheel. "So, do you want to get lunch first when we get there?"

"Before riding the Ferris wheel?" She made a show of considering his idea. "It's really tall, you know."

He started the engine and glanced over at her. "It sounds like there's a dare in there somewhere."

"Maybe a little one."

He pulled away from the curb. "I think I can handle it."

She gave him a good look as his attention was on the road in front of him. His hands looked big, even on the large leather-wrapped steering wheel. His seat was way back, to accommodate his long legs. He filled the space, and so did his fresh scent. Sort of minty, but warm.

"You look like you can handle just about anything, Graham Cracker."

She didn't know why she'd said that, since her face was now flaming hot. He didn't look at her, but she saw his cheek curve with an obvious smile.

"Trying to tempt me, Cupcake?"

She couldn't answer him. Her heart was hammering as her body flushed hot and cold. Her slime ball radar might not be buzzing but she felt something humming between them. Something that she'd never felt before. She took in a deep breath and let it out slowly.

She could do this. She could date this delicious-looking guy and keep things light and easy. If she started wanting more? She'd make sure to keep that a deep dark secret he would never discover.

After what had happened with Brad, she wasn't up for anything more.

Chapter 5

What the hell had he said to put that worried expression on her face? They'd been bantering, after all. Teasing back and forth as he steered them toward their date. Then she'd gotten spooked by something. There was no way he'd ask her what was wrong, though. Nope.

He made his living talking a good game, so instead of talking about feelings or anything sticky like that he tapped into his talent to fill the space as they drove. Little by little, she seemed to ease until a huge Ferris wheel appeared up ahead.

"There it is," she said.

"Pretty hard to miss."

She laughed a little and seemed to lose that last bit of stiffness. He found a parking space set near a towering human-sling-shot thing and faced her. "Ready to hit it?"

"Sure."

They got out and he saw that the place looked pretty cool. There were brick-paved streets closed off to everything but foot traffic, and all of the shops and restaurants were painted to look like individual buildings even though were connected. There was one store selling T-shirts with just about every current pop-culture phrase you could think of and a store that sold island-themed stuff like coconut heads and clothes that would fit in at a parrot-head concert.

He saw an old-fashioned general store that had barrels of penny candy and a soda fountain. Thrill rides like zip lines and more of those slingshot things towered overhead, not to mention that gigantic Ferris wheel. Restaurants with bar top seating were interspersed with New Age crystal shops and stores selling homemade soaps and creams.

He stuck his hands in his pockets as they strolled side by side on the brick walk. If felt like a place where you'd hold hands, and he so wasn't a hand-holder.

"When was the last time you were here?" he asked her.

She shrugged. "I don't know. A couple of years maybe? They've really grown, and it looks like they've been fixing the place up."

The buildings did look freshly-painted and the village looked pretty clean.

"It reminds me of Faneuil Hall up in Boston. Shops and touristy stuff, but with a whole different vibe."

"Did you grow up in Boston?"

"Yeah." His answer was short, and he hoped that would discourage her from asking anything else about his childhood. It wasn't a pretty story. "You grew up in Florida, right?"

"Yes, but not in Cypress Corners. We lived up in Orlando, where my dad's law practice is."

"I've seen a lot of commercials for lawyers, not to mention billboards. Florida seems to have a ton of them."

She laughed lightly. "We do. About one hundred thousand, actually."

He whistled. "Man. Glad I'm on the right side of the law."

Looking at him out of the corner of her eye, she smirked. "No back-alley deals, Eli? No under-the-table stuff to make a sale?"

He held out his arms. "I am always honest and above board."

She faced him, tilting her head to one side. "You know, I think I believe you."

"Well believe it, baby. I don't need to do anything underhanded." He tapped his chest. "Pure talent."

Now she laughed a little more. "Graham Cracker, you're a riddle."

"Nay. I'm an open book. Just like I told Mrs. Rollins."

"Hmm. And just what did Becky's mom want to know about you?"

"Seems to me she knew everything already. I'm from Boston. I'm going to be working at the Sales Center. There's a grapevine in Cypress, I think."

"Yes, and the queen of the vineyard is Lettie Fairfax. Have you met her yet?"

He searched his memory for the faces he'd seen in Cypress last spring. "I don't think so."

Her eyes sparkled. "She's going to love you."

"Do I want to know what you mean by that?"

"She's a Southern woman of a certain age, Eli. That doesn't stop her from eyeing every guy between seventeen and seventy, though."

"Brutal. Should I be worried?"

"Not at all. She's outrageous and can sniff out a secret in the wink of an eye, though."

"Again, I'm open and above board. No secrets here."

Caro seemed to take him at his word. He did have secrets, though. Dark, lonely ones that he'd fought long and hard to put behind him. Luckily, a little storefront claiming they had over one hundred flavors of popcorn was just up ahead on their right.

"It's a little early, but how do you feel about buffalo popcorn, Cupcake?"

She wrinkled her nose. "Hmm. Popcorn sounds good, but maybe not that one."

He opened the door for her and a little bell jingled overhead. "That's cute, but I like your door chime better."

"I thought it would be fun." She walked up to the long glass case filled with round bins of popcorn in a rainbow of colors. "I needed some fun when I first opened."

He nodded as they peered into the case. "Was it tough in the beginning?"

She bit her lip. "I struggled for about a year before taking the plunge."

"When did you take it? The plunge, I mean?"

"Just over two years ago. That first year was a doozy."

"You survived, Cupcake. Flourished, it looks like."

She beamed a smile and he was nearly knocked back on his ass by the beauty of it. "Thanks. I have."

"Would you like to sample some flavors?" the teenage kid behind the counter asked them in a cracking voice.

Eli looked at Caro, who nodded.

"Yes!" She peered through the glass again. "Ooh, how about pumpkin spice?"

"Pumpkin spice popcorn?" Eli asked.

Caro laughed at him. "Live a little, Graham Cracker."

"All right." Eli winked at her. "Buffalo, please."

The kid handed them each a tiny paper cup with a few pieces of their chosen popcorn. Caro moaned a little as she crunched hers and he had no choice but to try his. His tongue burned and his eyes watered.

"Mmm, this is delicious." Caro eyed him. "You okay there, Eli?"

"Yeah." He coughed. "Wow."

"It's hot," the kid stated.

Eli leveled a look at him. "Yeah," he said again.

"Oh, I think I need a bag of this," Caro said. "How about yours?"

"No, thanks." Eli tossed his little cup into the nearest trash can. "I'm good."

"A big bag of the pumpkin spice, please."

The kid passed her a big paper bag full of the stuff and Eli waved her hand away when she tried to pay. "My treat."

"Thanks." She munched a couple more pieces before holding it out to him. "Want to try it?"

He doubted he could taste anything after that fire popcorn. He smiled. "Maybe later."

"I think I might want to do something like this at the bakery," she said as they stepped back out onto the brick walk.

"What, flavored popcorn?"

"Sure. Maybe for a garnish? I'll have to talk to Jane about it."

"Who's Jane?"

"My assistant. She's amazing. If she doesn't have a recipe in hand she can create one."

"Has she been with you from the beginning?"

Caro nodded. "And Sweet Escape wouldn't be what it is without her."

"I look forward to meeting her the next time I come in."

"The next time?"

"I've got a sweet tooth, remember?"

"And yet you tried the buffalo popcorn."

"That was purely a guy thing. I had to prove my manhood."

She shook her head with a little smile. "With popcorn?"

He shrugged and shoved his hands in his pockets. "We do what we can, Cupcake."

There was a fifties-style diner a few doors from the popcorn store, and he steered her toward it. Silver and red and very shiny, it looked like it could be fun. After all, fun was one of the words of the day.

"How about some lunch?" he asked. "If you've had enough of that popcorn for now."

"Oh, I don't think I'll ever have enough of this, but I could eat lunch."

He pulled open the heavy glass door and waved her ahead of him into the black-and-white tiled, sparkly vinyl covered restaurant.

***

Their walk through the rest of Old Town Village was easy and comfortable. She reasoned that anyone looking at them would never guess that this was their first date.

They'd had a good meal at the diner and a good time after lunch, too. They'd played Skee-ball and other games in the arcade. They'd browsed the gift shops and clothing stores, and laughed at the ridiculous sayings scrawled across fake license plates and plaques. Talk was easy and light, and just what she needed today. *He* was just what she needed, and she tried hard not to feel any apprehension about that fact. It had been a long time since she'd needed a guy.

"How about it, Cupcake?"

They'd stopped and she followed his gaze up toward the top of the huge Ferris wheel. Her belly twisted a little bit.

She hesitated. "Um."

"Are you afraid of heights?"

"No, not really." She watched as the wheel turned. The gondolas rose slowly to the top, and then seemed to hang for a few seconds to swing back and forth. "It's just that ride back down that gets me every time."

"Ah, baby." He grabbed her hand, and it felt like the most natural thing in the world. "I'll be right there by your side."

Her belly twist started to turn, but she suspected that was due to Eli holding her hand. Due to the thought of being so close to him in one of those open-air gondolas of the wheel.

They waited their turn and Eli handed her up into the gondola. The bucket rocked back and forth as he settled down beside her and she caught her breath. He grinned at her and sat back, holding on to one side of the bucket.

"Ready for a ride, Cupcake?"

He was stretched out, filling the space with his big body and long legs. Their hips touched and she didn't make a move to change that. It was daylight, after all. They were in a public place. She was in no danger to throwing herself at him no matter how cute he looked with those pretty blue eyes of his sparkling like crystalized sugar.

"I'm ready, Graham Cracker."

They moved upward as others took their places in their own gondolas. Rocking to a stop each time, they made their way toward the top. This part of the ride, facing into the gears and spokes of the wheel, wasn't so bad. It was that ride down with the wheel at her back that made her a little nervous.

She grabbed onto his very strong bicep as they reached the top. He tensed for a second, and then released the side rail to cover her hand with his. They stopped at the top now, rocking gently as people got on somewhere way below them.

"Look," he said, tilting his chin.

She did, seeing that the sky was clear and the view was spectacular. "Oh!"

The city spread out, and they could see everything toward the big theme parks, the oaks and palm trees, the lakes and wilderness. It was everything in one fell swoop, and was Central Florida in a nutshell.

"You haven't been on this in a while, I take it."

There was laughter in his voice, and she couldn't help but smile. "Not in a long while, no. This view, Eli."

"I know." His lips parted. "It's like a dream."

"That's it exactly," she said.

Then they started to move downward, seemingly freefalling as the wheel turned as they made their way. No one else was boarding, apparently. There was no pause, no jerking stops, as they rode upward again.

The breeze pushed her hair all around, tangling around both her and Eli. He gently grasped a thick strand, tucking it behind her ear as he leaned in. It felt so right to kiss him. That teasing, flirting mouth looked so good. Better than one of her best cupcakes.

"Caro," he rasped, his lips a hairsbreadth away from hers. "I'm going to kiss you. Okay?"

She licked her lips, already anticipating him. "God, yes," she breathed.

He chuckled and covered her lips with his. She closed her eyes, grabbing more tightly to him as she angled her head to taste him.

He felt so good held tight against her, strong and solid and warm. He'd made her feel safe, although they were only in artificial danger. So she just opened her mouth and let him inside.

He groaned, his hands on her hips as his tongue teased hers. It was the single best kiss of her life, and that errant thought was almost sad as she was just three years shy of thirty.

Pulling back a fraction, he brought his brow to hers and sighed. "Damn, you taste good."

"You too," she managed to say in return.

He dropped a sweet kiss on her lips and sat up. She noticed then that they were stopped again. Not quite at the top of the wheel, but nearly.

"The ride is almost over," she said.

He flashed that bright smile again. "Ah, Cupcake. The ride is just beginning."

His words sent tingles all through her. Her cheeks hot, she took some time to gather her wild curls into some kind of order as they made their inevitable descent.

He held her hand as they stepped out of the gondola, and didn't release her until they reached his SUV. After he unlocked the car with the key fob, they got into the car and he started it up, opening the windows to let out the heat that had accumulated as the A/C blew hard.

"This was fun, Caro. We'll have to come back at night some time."

"They have classic car shows almost every Friday and Saturday night," she said. "And the view from the top of the wheel would be incredible!"

He dragged his gaze over her. "It's pretty good from where I'm sitting."

She laughed. "Do you have a book of those lines, Eli?"

He winked as he pulled out of the space. "I don't need a book."

She shook her head but couldn't help but smile wider as he drove them back to Cypress.

Eli was a contradiction, but a pretty hot one at that. He was easy and fun, which should have been the opposite of the Alpha male she'd grabbed a hold of on the Ferris wheel and then let kiss her senseless. There seemed to be more beneath his curt statement about his childhood in Boston, too. He'd been short and not very forthcoming. It felt strange and out of character, since he gave off that open-book vibe. But she wasn't going to be the one to pry.

She had her own secrets that would stay shut tight in her own book, thank you very much.

Chapter 6

Eli was up with the sun again. He showered and dressed, choosing a light gray dress shirt and slate blue tie. A power tie, of course. He put on a pair of pressed chinos, as that seemed to be the unofficial uniform for the executives at the Sales Center. The other guys in sales dressed in polos and relaxed khakis, but he always bought into the adage to dress for the job you want. He wasn't eyeing Rick Chapman's job. He wouldn't do anything to step on any toes, either. He simply wanted to be the best sales guy wherever he worked, either here in Cypress Corners or back up in Boston.

Today he would start working at the Sales Center, and he suspected Bill Chapman would soon call or email with his marching orders. There were a lot of projects in the works, from the green community currently under construction and minimally occupied. Bill wanted to make sure he had a hand in the Active Adult project, though.

Eli knew he could sell the place sight unseen, but he had to learn what he could. He also had to sell the whole concept of Cypress, too. And that meant lots of meetings and tours over the next few days, if not weeks.

His phone dinged, and he saw he had a notification from

Rick. It was his schedule for the day. He would take a tour of the eco sides of things with Ty Walsh at ten. Then he was to shadow the other sales people throughout the day, Oliver and Sabrina and Jessie. Then at two o'clock there was a meeting with the staff called by Mr. Forbes, the developer. Eli was glad now that he was dressed for battle, so to speak.

He clicked on the links to confirm the list of appointments and pocketed his phone as he took a glance around his guest room. This place would be good for now. If he wasn't summoned back to Boston any time soon, though? He'd have to figure out something a little more permanent. He'd lived out of a suitcase, or sometimes out of a backpack or a box tucked under a bed, for most of his life. His apartment in Boston wasn't a permanent place. He was renting six months at a time, and starting to get tired of it. Even his furniture was on lease.

Shutting out thoughts about his transient life, he left his room and went down to the lobby. The innkeeper stood just inside the dining room.

"Good morning, Mrs. Rollins."

"Good morning, Mr. Graham," Mrs. Rollins said with a smile. "And good luck today."

"Thank you." He went into the dining room and made

himself a coffee to go. He saw a tray holding cinnamon rolls tucked into little brown bags. There weren't as many on display as there had been on the weekend. If someone stayed here during the week, they would probably be up and out early. Cypress Corners wasn't a lazy place, after all. The weekends were for fun; the weekdays for work.

After debating for a second, he grabbed one of the packaged pastries. "Don't tell Sweet Escape," he said with a wink.

Mrs. Rollins laughed and winked back at him. "My lips are sealed."

Yeah, I'll just bet.

Thoughts of Caro and that amazing kiss struck him then. She'd been a little hot and cold during their conversations as they'd strolled through Old Town Village, but when they were on the Ferris Wheel? Nothing but smokin' hot, in his opinion.

He ate the roll as he went out to his car, and sipped his coffee as he drove the less than two miles to the Sales Center. Parking his SUV in the adjacent lot, he got out and strolled down the short path to the wide front steps. It was a cool morning, but the tall trees bordering the golf course across the main street were still a bright green. Autumn in Cypress Corners was still summer, it seemed.

The coffee shop beckoned from across the street, and he tossed his half-finished cup of mediocre brew into the nearest trash can. As he entered the courtyard of the shop he smiled at the older woman seated by herself at a table beneath a flowering tree.

"Yoo-hoo!" she called with a finger-wiggling wave.

Eli stopped at her table and dipped his head. "Good morning."

"You must be our newest young man to settle into Cypress Corners. I'm Charlotte Fairfax, but you can call me Lettie."

An alarm dinged in his head and he remembered all Caro had said about this woman. Lettie was as she'd described her, but she'd left out the big hat and denim smock. Her twinkling blue eyes narrowed on him from beneath her fringe of silvery bangs. Ah, here was the woman who could sniff out a secret.

"It's a pleasure to meet you, Lettie. I'm Eli Graham."

"Oh I know that, dear boy." She folded her hands. "You're working for Rick Chapman over at the Sales Center."

He stroked a hand down his tie as he took in a breath. "Yes ma'am, that's right."

Her brows rose and her lips pursed. "Ooh, you're quite a

gentleman. For a Yankee, that is."

He laughed. "I try my best."

"Your mother must have raised you right."

A chill wormed through him and his smile faltered. "Yes."

"You know, Eli. I believe Cypress Corners is the absolute best place in the world to live. I should know. I've traveled the world with the late Mr. Fairfax."

"It seems like a very nice place."

"Now you pour on that charm when you give your tours, you hear? Show people how they can be happier here than anywhere else."

"That's the plan."

"You know, you can be happy here too."

He stiffened, but in the next second his usual ease washed over him. "I've enjoyed myself so far."

"Mmm hmm. I've heard that, too."

So she knew about his date with Caro. Well, he wasn't going to talk to her about it. Not when he'd just been thinking about that kiss.

"I'm going to grab myself a cup of coffee and then get to work. May I get you anything, Lettie?"

"No, dear boy." She held up her cup. "I have my sweet tea

right here."

He queued up and got himself a cup of coffee before crossing back through the courtyard with merely a nod to Lettie. Her innocent comment about his mother shouldn't have bothered him but he barely remembered his mother. From what little he'd been told about her? He doubted she'd done any kind of raising, let alone the right way. Pushing those thoughts out of his head, he climbed the few wide steps up to the front doors of the Sales Center.

"Good morning, Eli!" A thin guy he vaguely remembered from his last visit bounced up the steps to join him at the front door. "Happy first day."

Eli smiled at the pretty guy. He was blond and had big blue eyes, and looked like a fit cherub. If Eli didn't miss his guess, he played for the other team.

"Thanks."

"Oliver." The guy held out his hand and Eli shook it. "We'll be working together a little today."

"Looking forward to it."

Oliver tilted his head to one side, eyeing Eli up and down. "Hmm. Another one. Just my luck."

"Another what?"

84

"Don't let him scare you," Rick Chapman said as he pushed the door open. "Ollie, don't you have a tour this morning?"

"Yes, Boss Man." Oliver winked at Eli. "I'm the number one sales person, now that Tammy's out on maternity leave."

Rick gave Oliver a small smile. "Maybe at the moment. Jessie is giving you a run for your money, though."

Oliver clicked his tongue and hurried through the lobby. "We'll see," he threw over his shoulder.

Rick shook his head and faced Eli. "I'm glad to have you on board, Eli."

"Thanks. Your father was very insistent, Mr. Chapman."

"Yeah, that's among Bill's many traits. And call me Rick."

"Thank you, Rick."

"This lovely lady is Sharon Walsh," Rick said, indicating an older woman behind the reception desk. "She job-shares three days a week, and the sales staff fills in as needed on the other days."

"Hello, Mrs. Walsh." He nodded. "Eli Graham."

"Hi there, Eli." She looked like a motherly lady, with light brown hair and kind hazel eyes. "I hope you'll like it here."

"I believe I will," he said.

"Let me show you where you'll be," Rick started down the hallway to the left.

Eli followed him down a corridor with opened doors. Brass name plaques were beside each of them, and he read them as he passed. Tammy Chapman. Claire Chapman. Ben Chapman.

"I'm seeing a trend," Eli observed with a smile.

"Yeah, it's kind of become a family business." Rick chuckled. "Surprised the hell out of me, too."

"I heard about Tammy and your brother's baby. Congratulations."

"Thanks. Little Raffaella is the latest, but Claire and my other brother Jake's little one won't be too far behind."

Eli just nodded. Kids and family were things he knew less than nothing about. To his relief, they soon arrived in a large room holding several workstations.

"This is the general sales area," Rick said. "You'll have your own work space, along with Oliver, Jessie and Sabrina."

"Bree." A pretty blond stood, flipping her long hair over one shoulder before holding out her hand. "It's just Bree. Hi, nice to see you again."

Eli shook her hand as he worked his mind. "Yeah, you were working out at one of the models in the green neighborhood when I was down here."

"Sure was," she said.

"You're here next to me, Eli," Oliver called.

Eli looked at Rick for confirmation, who gave him a nod.

"Go ahead and get settled in," Rick said. "You'll find everything you need in that folder. Log-in credentials, key card, etc."

Eli placed his hand flat on the glossy green folder bearing the Cypress Corners logo. The long-necked bird on the logo seemed to be staring at him. "Thanks."

"Jessie should be in in a little while," Rick went on. "She can give you any info you need on the conservation side of things."

"So this is another wild tour?"

"An eco-tour, yes. It will be a lot more detailed than the one you and Derek took when you were here last."

Eli grinned. "Ah. So this is more than just keeping me busy this time?"

"You were working for my father when you were down here, Eli. After you sign your W-4s? You'll be working for Cypress Corners."

Eli blinked. He hadn't thought about that, but legally he'd

be tied to Cypress. Not to Bill. Suddenly he felt a little adrift. Nodding mutely, he settled at the indicated desk and booted up the laptop resting there.

"I'll leave you to it." Rick nodded at Oliver and Bree. "Don't forget, Mr. Forbes called for a meeting today at two."

"We've got it, Boss Man," Oliver said.

Eli simply nodded. This was strange. He was in this big room with colleagues, which he could handle. His ego wasn't so big that he couldn't coexist with the other salespeople. The place felt both personal and professional, which seemed to be in opposition, but the numbers didn't lie. The Sales Center was very successful, and success bred success in his book. A rising tide lifts all boats, after all.

Setting his unease aside, he synced his phone to the Cypress Corners closed internet and drained the rest of his coffee. New log-ins, new office space, new coworkers.

Today was going to be the first for a lot of things, apparently.

***

Caro brushed her hair back from her face and folded her arms. Sweet Escape had been pretty busy today, but it was closing time now. She was nearly finished cleaning up out here while Jane prepped a few things in the kitchen for tomorrow morning.

She'd been glad for the business today, and for more than the obvious reasons. Her date with Eli yesterday had been fun and easy, just as he'd predicted. At least on the surface, anyway. There was the little matter of that sky-high kiss.

Oh, he'd tasted so good. And his strong arms had felt so nice wrapped around her as they'd gone round and round. She wasn't stupid, though. He was a flirt, and he had only just come to Cypress Corners. Who knew what the heck he was looking for? She wouldn't worry about whether or not she was the answer to that question. She was so not ready for anything that close. That emotional.

"Ready to hit it?" Jane asked with a smile.

She'd obviously dropped her dirty apron into the bin for the laundry service. Caro nodded and untied her own, shorter apron. "Thanks for today, Jane. You're a godsend."

"I know it." Jane gave her usual short laugh. "Are you going to tell me what has you looking so concerned?"

"It's nothing."

"Should I be worried?"

Caro shook her head. "Not at all. I'm just thinking."

"Maybe you're just tired?"

"Probably."

"Big date yesterday?"

Caro blinked. "Huh?"

Jane waved a hand. "I heard that you took a little trip to Old Town Village with a certain blond god."

"Who told you?"

"Well, I heard it from Tom when I went next door to get my macchiato. He must have heard from Becky."

Caro shook her head. "Becky wouldn't tell her little brother a thing, Jane. It had to be that nosy mother of theirs."

"Maybe. That woman should just pull up a chair and sit with Lettie."

"So now I'm the latest gossip fodder?" Caro rolled her eyes. "Fantastic."

"Not gossip, Caro." Jane's gaze was soft. "People were just remarking. They've had nothing to talk about since Ben and Tammy had their baby."

"Well that's just their too bad, isn't it?" Caro took in a breath, deep and slow, and let it out. "I don't know what the big deal is anyway. It was just one date."

"True." Jane tilted her head. "Do you want more than just

one date?"

"He's a nice guy, Jane. He's fun, and let's face it. He's very easy on the eyes."

"He's hot, Caro. Smokin' hot. I'm old enough to be his mother and I'm still saying that."

Caro smiled a little. "I'm not blind, Jane."

"Or dead either, though you're acting like it."

"Please, not this again? I haven't even wanted to date much since the accident."

"The accident wasn't what did you in, Caro. It was finding out what an ass hat you were about to marry. I think God did you a solid there. Sucked that the jerk had to die, though."

God, she loved Jane's no-nonsense personality. Brad was a shit, and losing her fiancé to a pop-up thunderstorm on a rainy road at the same time she'd learned he'd been cheating on her? The two combined to mess her up but good. Not to mention the other.

She unconsciously splayed a hand over her midsection before dropping it to her side. "I definitely don't want to talk about that, thanks."

"Then let's call it a day." Jane slipped off her crocs and slammed her bike helmet on her head. "See you at oh dark thirty tomorrow."

Caro laughed. "Four thirty will be fine. Heck, make it five."

"And have you show me up? Nuh uh."

Jane left, riding her bike home to her house in one of the more densely-populated villages of Cypress. She and her husband were empty-nesters, not like Caro's poor parents. They did stuff together and on their own, comfortable that the other would always be there.

Her parents were like that as well, and their nest was nearly empty, though. It wasn't that Caro didn't want her own place. She just was leery of taking that step. Today of all days, she didn't want to think about why.

Caro glanced out one of the picture windows toward the Sales Center across the street. Eli started working there today. She wondered how his day had gone. Pretty easy, she could imagine. He looked capable and his personality would help him fit in just about anywhere. She might have only spent part of a day with him, but she imagined he could handle himself in just about any situation.

"So not like me," she murmured.

She couldn't resist a shot of caffeine, so after a quick stop into the coffee shop for an iced pumpkin spice latte she got into her mini and drove back to her parents' place. After she parked and turned off the motor, she sat for a long minute. As the temperature started to climb inside the little car, she grabbed her coffee and just starting walking.

The main lakeshore across the street beckoned, but the kids were just getting out at the community school at this hour and she couldn't deal with that at the moment. Turning, she headed for the dock that marked the border of the private beach of the Cypress Inn.

She might tease Becky's mother about the cinnamon rolls and her gossip, but the woman was sweet and never minded when Caro hung out in the space regularly reserved for guests. The raised wooden walk made its way toward a point which afforded a fantastic view of the huge lake. The end of the walk was framed with a pergola-style roof semi-open to the sky and a rough-hewn bench swing suspended by sturdy chains. A few tall, broad trees gave her a bit of dappled shade, and she settle down in the swing. One leg folded up under her and the other draped down to toe the swing into gentle motion. At last she gave in to the emotions that she'd pressed back since she'd woken up this morning.

Squeezing her eyes shut, she felt hot tears seep through her lashes. She didn't mourn Brad any longer. She hadn't in truth, not after learning just what he'd been up to for months before the accident. Her mother and sister had handled the logistics of cancelling the various venders and things regarding the wedding that would never be, and Caro had gotten through his funeral in a state of cold removal. It was what had happened a week after that, three years to the day today, that had caused her to pull into herself.

She'd never had the chance to tell Brad she was pregnant. No one in her family, none of her friends, had known either. It had been so very new, shiny and exciting and heart-stopping when she'd read the positive result on that little pink stick. So there was no one to tell when the baby was no more.

Her OBGYN had confirmed her fear, and that she'd been about three weeks along. The doctor had assured her that she could certainly get pregnant again, as there didn't appear to be anything in Caro's physiology to indicate that her miscarriage was anything but stress-related. Like when she'd lost Brad, or the dream of marriage to Brad, she'd had mixed feelings. Certainly it was a relief that she wouldn't have this last tie to that cheating bastard. But she'd begun to dream about her little sweetheart before losing him or her, and still felt so hollow inside today.

Sniffling, she put her coffee down on the decking and covered her face with her hands and cried. Cried for her baby and cried for herself. She wasn't alone. She had friends and family who loved her. But in this?

In her sorrow, she was completely alone.

Chapter 7

"So did we scare you away?" Rick asked.

Eli looked up from his laptop screen at his new boss. "Not at all. You're stuck with me, for a while at least."

"Good. My father might have suggested you but today I saw a little of what he sees. You're sharp, Eli. You're smart and have a way with people. That's what we need."

Eli swallowed past the sudden, unwelcome lump in his throat. "Thank you, Rick."

"A few of us are headed to the tavern for dinner, if you don't have any plans."

Eli's mind worked. The bakery was closed. He'd seen that when he'd returned from his last tour of the day. It was just after five now, and he had nowhere to go.

"I'll pass tonight, but thanks," he told Rick.

Rick nodded. "Then I'll say have a good night."

Eli went back to his screen. He'd been thumbing through the listings of available rentals in Cypress, and a townhouse popped up. He figured it would suit him better than a house.

"Hey, Jessie?" He turned in his chair to find the Pixie typing furiously on her laptop. "Can I ask you something?"

"Mmm hmm." She took off her pink-framed glasses and

Dreaming Eli ~ JoMarie DeGioia

faced him. "What's up?"

"You live in one of the townhouses, right?"

"I do. We're renting Tammy's old place, actually."

"How do you like it?"

A smile broke out across her pretty face. "I love it. Noah and I have made a nice home there. For Max and for us."

"Max?"

"Noah's son. Our son, now."

Eli blinked. He didn't know the story, but he figured there had to be one there. He wasn't one to pry, though. Or to gossip.

"Why do you ask?" Jessie went on.

"There's one available to rent. I'm thinking about grabbing it."

"And moving out of the inn?" She nodded. "Good for you."

Eli leaned back and folded his arms. "I'm not sure, but I think it's worth looking into."

Jessie put her glasses back on and tapped on her laptop. "Which unit is it?"

"It's the end unit across from the golf course."

She laughed softly. "It must be the other end of our building, then. About five doors down from us."

"Is that a problem?"

She looked up again. "Why would that be a problem?"

"Your husband isn't my biggest fan."

She waved a hand. "That's when he thought you were flirting with me."

Eli nearly choked. "He thought what?"

"Back in the spring, Eli. It's no big, and I never felt creeped out by you."

He grinned. "That's what all the ladies say."

Oliver barked a laugh as he joined them in the general sales room. "Good one, Eli."

"Thanks, Oliver."

"So are you coming to the tavern?" Oliver asked.

"I don't think so."

Oliver shrugged. "Well, congrats on surviving your first day."

Eli shut down his computer and stood. "Yep. Alligators and wild boars on the eco-tour couldn't scare me away. I think I can face working with you all."

He left his new coworkers and headed out to his vehicle. The day was still warm but it seemed less humid than it had been just a couple of hours earlier. At the stop sign he had a clear

98

view of the Clubhouse and Town Tavern, but he wasn't tempted to change his mind. He wasn't used to working so closely with other salespeople, so Rick's survival question hadn't been too far off the mark.

When he'd first gotten into sales, he'd been too focused to foster relationships with coworkers. Everything was kept solely on the surface, which helped him keep his head on straight as he worked toward a general education Bachelor's degree from a small community college in Boston. That had taken him five years since he'd had to work full-time as well. Sales fit his schedule, and commissions paid his tuition and other bills.

He'd been thrown out of the foster care system and was lucky enough to land right into a job for one of his old foster fathers. That job, working at an electronics store, taught him how to read people. How to upsell, which was not as dirty a word as someone not in sales might assume. He never pushed anything on a customer if he didn't think they would be happy with the purchase. That went for the smallest digital camera to the biggest whole-house sound system. Then he found himself in real estate, and started to diversify his particular set of skills.

He was grateful to Bill Chapman for taking a chance on him three years ago. He'd worked his ass off, learning everything about what made his boss successful and his company grow ever larger. Sales turned into retaining accounts, which was just as important in a business that could turn on a dime. With no one to answer to at home, no steady girlfriends, no close friends at all really, he could devote all the time Bill needed from him. Now, though? Working in a place like Cypress? Slowing his roll would take some getting used to. That was for sure.

He turned left at the stop and headed toward the nearest village of townhouses. The unit he was considering was less than a mile from the town center, which meant he could walk to work when the sweaty season was over. He reached over to crank up the A/C. Like in December.

The townhouses looked like separate residences, which appealed to him. Classic details were evident in this village as well. Columns and railings framed the porches and deep eaves gave the homes a rich look. They appeared to be pretty big, too. It was little wonder that units seldom came on the market for sale. Even if you didn't want to live in it yourself, it made a whole lot of sense to rent it out. With the golf course, nature, the schools and other amenities rents were pretty healthy. The one he was looking at would rent for nearly two grand a month.

The end unit he saw first had to be Jessie and Noah's. It looked so homey and welcoming, with a bench seat holding plump pillows and a big leafy wreath on the glossy front door. He didn't miss the little fairies or whatever decorating their tiny front yard, either.

Their neighbors also seemed settled into their units, except for the end unit he was considering. It looked like a mirror of Jessie and Noah's, but it was lacking any sort of homey vibe. Just a porch without a wreath, mat or bench. Nothing in the yard but the same shrubs as the others on the street. The white plantation blinds were shut and the house had a sleepy look. An empty look.

Disappointment pooled in his belly, but he beat it back.

He'd had enough of the foolish dream that this time, this foster home, would be a real home. He'd never been abused, thank God, but he'd never been loved either. He'd been tolerated. Sheltered. Fed. It didn't take much thinking for him to know why he'd never figured out how to make a home. So he never had one. He hadn't felt this longing since he was a kid. And right now? Right now it pissed him the hell off.

Stopping the truck, he set the brake. The unit was over two thousand square feet. Three beds, two and a half baths. Open concept with a large kitchen and great room, dining area and dedicated office space. It ticked off a lot of boxes for anybody looking for a home in Cypress. The real question was, was he?

He started the engine and continued on to the Cypress Inn. It was a very nice place. It was comfortable and didn't need anything from him to make it livable. It was pretty but impersonal, just like the women he'd bedded in the last few years. Hell, that was getting old too. He felt restless, and banging a stranger wasn't the answer it had been in the past. Not the bartender at the tavern or the server at the sports bar had tempted him. He probably should try to figure out why, but he was a little afraid of what the answer might be.

He parked and walked around the inn toward the main lakeshore. This parcel of land, beach and woods, was private for the inn's guests. That was a relief, since he wouldn't have to make small talk with anyone like he would if he'd gone to the tavern with the others from the Sales Center. He could hear voices from further to the east, from the soccer field and the playground near the larger beach. Kids. Families. So not his scene.

Loosening his tie, he pulled it off and coiled it around his hand before stuffing it in his front pocket. Lifting his chin, he undid a few shirt buttons and began to roll up his sleeves. He'd take a page from Oliver and Rick tomorrow, and wear something a little softer. A little easier. Something that wouldn't wrinkle as he drove one of the golf carts around through the hot and humid days to come.

He caught sight of one of the raised wooden walkways and made his way through the primitive-looking trees. Spanish moss dripped off the cypress and oaks here, too. Spikey plants nestled at the bases of the trees, and the ground looked boggy as he neared the lake. Then it opened up to a small deck set beneath a pergola that had an unobstructed view of the glistening lake. He heard a soft sound and turned, realizing then that he wouldn't have the view to himself.

There, tucked into the wooden swing and clearly asleep, was Caro Richmond.

***

"Caro?" Eli asked.

Caro shifted, wondering why Eli was in her bedroom. Not that she wouldn't like to see him in her bedroom someday…

"Hey, Cupcake." His voice was teasing now. Cajoling.

A big hand grasped her shoulder and gave her a gentle shake. She awoke with a start, and then hissed out a breath as pins and needles danced up and down her leg. She wasn't in her bedroom. She was out at the lake. She'd dozed off there on the swing, and her leg beneath her had fallen asleep too.

Cursing softly, she shifted and rubbed at her thigh. She looked up at Eli then, blinking as the sun bounced off of him like it did the lake.

"Eli, what are you doing here?"

"I came to do some thinking, I guess. You?"

"The same."

Her eyes felt gritty and her throat raw. Grabbing up her diluted iced coffee, she took a long sip. She remembered then what she'd blocked out all day. What she'd come here to think about and finally give in to the cry she'd denied herself.

Eli leaned against the railing in front of her, crossing his big arms. "It doesn't look like the thoughts were very good ones."

Tears pricked at her eyes again. She bit her lip and set her cup back down. Swallowing her tears, she shook her head. "I fell asleep, I guess. It's so peaceful out here."

He nodded. "It is."

He continued to stare at her and she slowly unfolded her leg to flex her muscles.

104

"My leg fell asleep, too," she said.

"How long have you been out here?"

"Since closing up shop, I guess. Why, what time is it?"

"Almost five thirty."

She gaped at him. "I've been out here two hours?"

"I suppose." He lifted his chin toward the swing. "Can I join you?"

Nodding, she shifted over to give him some room. "How did your first day go?"

He gave her a crooked smile. "Oh no, you don't. Why don't you tell me what sent you out here, Cupcake? And why you were crying."

Her hands went to her cheeks and she felt the dried and salty tracks of tears there. Chapped lips and spiky lashes finished what she was sure was a lovely picture this evening.

"It's nothing," she whispered.

"I don't believe you." He sat back, his long legs stretching out toward the railing as he pushed them gently back and forth. "But you don't have to tell me. I'm not that guy."

She eyed him. "What guy?"

"The guy who pries into other people's business. Something happened today to upset you and you needed time

105

alone. I get that."

He was looking at her so openly, not pushing or demanding a thing from her. She felt she had to at least set a little bit of the record straight.

"It doesn't have anything to do with today, Eli. It's something that happened three years ago." She sucked in a breath. "Three years ago today, actually."

He gave her a slow nod. "And it's something that you don't want to talk about."

"No, I don't." She rubbed her cheeks and sniffled. "Don't take it personally. I've never talked about it with anyone."

He appeared thoughtful, his brows drawn together over his eyes. "Sounds serious."

"It is. It...was."

Turning, he came closer to her. "If you ever do want to talk about it, I'm sure your guy then. I know how to keep a secret."

"Really?" She felt a smile curve her lips. "I thought you were an open book."

"Ah, I'm open all right. That doesn't mean I can't keep somebody else's secret."

"I guess." She looked him over again, and breathed in some of his fresh spice scent. "This is a very strange conversation, Eli."

"Yeah?"

"Yes, and I feel like I'm missing something."

"I missed something today."

He was staring at her now, those crystal-sugar blue eyes of his doing twisty things to her insides.

"What?" she breathed.

He leaned closer. "You."

She pulled back. "Another line?"

"No line, Cupcake. I'm dead serious." He stroked a finger over her cheek, down the side of her neck and just under the collar of her T-shirt. "All day long I've been wanting a taste of what I had before."

She licked her lips and saw that he watched her mouth now. Oh, their kiss. "What was that?"

He brought his mouth close to her throat and breathed in before his lips teased her skin. "I craved another taste of those amazing brownies."

She gasped and then laughed. "Eli!"

He pulled back a bit and grinned at her. "That kiss yesterday was pretty sweet too, though."

She put her hands on his shoulders and shook her head.

"Mmm, I could use some sweet right now."

He growled softly and brought that teasing mouth to hers. His kiss was deep from the start, his lips fitting so perfectly to hers as his tongue slipped inside her mouth. Her sorrow forgotten for at least this moment, she pressed herself against him as he held her closer.

"Caro, you smell so good." His face was in the hollow of her throat now, that slight stubble of his just rough enough on her skin. "I want to taste you all over."

Ooh, this man. It had been so long since she'd been with a guy, she nearly melted at his words. One or two bad bedroom romps following one or two bad dates was the sum and total of her sexual life for the last three years. Eli wouldn't be like that, though. Clearly the guy knew everything he was doing to her. From his big hands on her butt to his tongue dancing over the pulse at the side of her neck.

"Come back to the inn with me," he said on a breath.

Her pulse raced at his words. She was so tempted. Tempted to wipe out the darkness of this day with some of his brightness. She'd only known him a couple of days, though. She wasn't built for one-night stands, which her romantic history proved.

"I can't," she whispered.

He turned, pressing against her so she could feel his whole body. He was hard everywhere, especially where she supposed it counted most. "Why not?"

Why not? Then it hit her. Reality, like a cold jump into the lake.

"You live at the inn, Eli." She dropped little kisses on his strong throat as she tried to find the strength to actually stop kissing him. "It would be all over town if I jumped into bed with you."

"So?"

"So?" She pulled back at last, tilted her head. "So? I'm just not—"

"That kind of girl?" he cut in with a wink.

"That's not what I was going to say. I'm just not ready for the stories to start again."

He bit that full lower lip of his. "Are you saying you have a past?"

"Not like whatever you're thinking."

He cupped her face and kissed her, tenderly this time. "I don't know what's going on with you, Cupcake. But know this. We're going to get together, baby. But I'm also not the guy to rush you."

She reached up and grasped his wrists in her hands, feeling his strength and wishing she could lean on him. For passion, sure. But for support.

"Thanks, Eli."

He stroked her cheeks with his thumbs before releasing her. "I saw an alligator today. Out on the eco-tour with Ty Walsh."

"Was it a big one?"

"Big enough, if you ask me. I'm a city boy, remember."

She nodded and gave a shiver. "Well, I'm not an outdoorsy girl so I'm with you there."

"Have you ever seen one?"

"You can't live in Cypress Corners and not see one. I even held one once."

His eyes widened. "Why?"

The horror on his face was almost laughable. "A guy from the gator place up in Orlando came out and had baby ones to hold. Their snouts were taped closed."

"That's better, I guess. What did that feel like? Holding a gator?"

She wrinkled her nose. "Like holding a hot purse."

He laughed. "I'll bet. So how about a pizza?"

Her stomach growled and she smiled. "I could eat."

"Apparently you could." Taking her hand in his, he tugged her to her feet. "Then let's leave all these deep thoughts and confessions here at the lake and go grab a pie at the tavern."

"Sounds good."

Chapter 8

Eli sat back, staring at the rental listing yet again. It was four o'clock Wednesday afternoon, and the Sales Center was quiet. Jessie worked at the Cypress Institute on Wednesdays and she was still across the street. Oliver was taking her tours while Bree covered the reception desk.

"What's got your panties in a twist?"

He smiled as Oliver sat himself down in Bree's chair at the desk next to Eli's. "No panties, Oliver."

Oliver's perfect brows arched over his wide blue eyes. "Going commando?"

Eli laughed out loud. "That's for me to know, and don't even think about finishing that sentence."

Oliver shrugged. "Hey, I have my own guy. I got so tired of wasting my fantasy life on you straight guys. It's like you're coming out of the woodwork around here."

"How did the tour go?"

"It was fine. Jessie was set to tour two older couples but only one showed."

Eli's ears perked up and his mind sharpened. "Older couples?"

"Yeah. The spry, healthy type. They wanted info on the

Active Adult community but we don't have any to give."

"Not yet, anyway."

Oliver straightened. "Do you know something, Eli?"

Eli gave a deliberate shake of his head. "Not me. I just started here."

"But you're from Chapman. You worked for the man himself, Bill the Great and Powerful."

"Really, Oliver?" Eli quirked a brow at him. "A Wizard of Oz reference?"

"Hey, if the curtain fits." Oliver jumped up again and peered at Eli's computer screen. "Still looking at that listing?"

"I think it would be a good move."

"You don't sound that excited about it."

"It's another rental."

"Another?"

Eli cleared his face and put on one of his go-to expressions of ease. "I just meant that my apartment in Boston is a rental."

Oliver stared at him for a long minute, but Eli wouldn't try to guess what he was looking for. He suspected this guy might appear light and easy, a lot like he himself pretended to be, but there was more there. Hell, as a gay man he had to have issues and concerns that Eli couldn't begin to imagine. He could appreciate them, though. Every guy was entitled to his own past, and to keep it to himself.

"I think you should take it," Oliver finally said.

"Yeah?"

"I know the homeowner. Moved out of state a few months ago and it doesn't look like he's coming back."

"And he's not going to sell, right?"

"Not now. Would you? Property values are only going up in our little hamlet."

"You live here too, then?"

"I do. Bought my own two-bedroom over on the backside of the townhouse village last year."

Pride was in Oliver's voice and Eli nodded. "Nice."

Oliver crossed his arms and struck a thoughtful pose. "Now I have to decide if Todd should move in or not."

"What's holding you back?"

"Todd isn't as…meticulous as I am."

"A little touch of OCD, Oliver?"

"I'm neat, Eli. Neat as a pin."

"And as prickly?"

Oliver laughed. "That's what Todd says!"

"Then I think you should definitely take the next step."

"The next step? Hmm. Maybe I will." Oliver pointed at Eli's computer. "How about you?"

Eli shrugged, eager to end this conversation. He was afraid that if he kept talking with Oliver he'd admit that he wanted to take the next step for the first time in his memory. Yeah, it was just renting a place, but it was here in Cypress Corners.

Oliver pulled out his phone and gave a dramatic gasp. "Gotta go spell Bree on the front desk!"

Eli waved absently as Oliver hurried out of the sales room. He felt like he was at a crossroads, and that was never a comfortable place for him in the past. Every time he showed up in another foster home, his ratty hand-me-down backpack holding a few clothes and not much else, he'd felt a mix of hope and worry. He'd never lasted anywhere very long. It was never anything he'd done. He'd made sure of that, with his mood and behavior. There always seemed to be some outside force taking away the dream of a forever place.

Not to be too maudlin, which was never his style, but something would inevitably happen to bring any current living situation to an end.

Maybe it was a divorce, which split up his foster parents. Or an upswing in their financial circumstances, which led to lessening the draw on their time once a foster parent could afford to cut a kid loose. There was even the time when a single foster mom met and married a guy who didn't like the idea of having a kid underfoot. Almost fifteen years in the system had left him counting his lucky stars, though. He'd never been in an abusive situation, and the kids he'd had to chill with in group homes now and then hadn't been so bad. He wasn't going to attend any foster family reunions any time soon, but he knew he was a lucky bastard.

Bastard. He was, and an orphan too. His parents had been teens, he'd been told. His father, or the kid his mother claimed had been his father, had cut and run before Eli was born. His mother had tried to raise him on her own. He had hazy memories of hugs and kisses, but not much else. She'd been a street kid, apparently. Maybe a former foster kid as well. No one had claimed Eli when she'd died of pneumonia that winter when he'd been three. Not his mother's family, wherever they might be. Not his possible father, who had been nowhere to be found.

They'd tried to find anyone in his family, or so he'd been told right before he'd aged out of the system. How hard they'd looked, he couldn't be sure. It hadn't mattered at that point, anyway. He was cut loose. He'd landed on his feet though, hadn't he?

"Sure as hell did," he muttered.

He glanced out the windows along one side of the sales room. It was bright and sunny out there, and way too nice a day to get nostalgic.

"Just do it, Eli," Jessie said as she breezed into the sales room. "You know you want to."

He found a smile for his possible neighbor. "I do?"

"You need a place. You have to get out of the inn."

"What's wrong with the inn, exactly?"

"Nothing. And the private beach is very nice. But man cannot live on cinnamon rolls alone."

He laughed now. "All right. I guess I need to get a place with a kitchen."

"You can cook?"

"I can cook enough, Jessie."

"Then do it! Because unless you want to live out in the tent-cabin, this is the best option right now."

He thought for a second about the little structure out by the far lakeshore. Cozy didn't begin to describe it. Even *he* would have a tough sell if that was one of his properties.

"Okay, you've sold me." He winked. "So to speak."

She clasped her hands, bouncing on the balls of her feet. "Good! I'll contact the homeowner and let him know. See if I can get you a friends and family discount."

Eli lost his smile but he nodded. "Thanks, Jessie."

He clicked out of the listing window and leaned back. Jessie was over at her desk now, talking in hushed tones but sounding perky and excited.

Cypress Corners, and the Sales Center for that matter, was so different from anything he'd known before. It wasn't just the weather, either. He glanced at his phone. He owed Bill a call, actually. But he had other considerations today. He was moving into Cypress. For real.

There was a big benefit to moving out of the inn that he couldn't ignore, though. If he rented this townhouse he wouldn't have the ever-observant innkeeper watching his every move. And then maybe he and Caro could finish what they'd started out by the lake, with no worries of anyone being any the wiser.

***

"Hey there, baker girl!"

Caro looked up with a smile as her friend Jessie Brady bounced into coffee shop. The place was almost empty at this hour, thank goodness. It was nearly four thirty, and Caro sat at a

118

table nursing her caramel macchiato. She was delaying going home. She'd gone straight home yesterday and her mother had dragged her downstairs and into another home style family dinner. Last night's had been chicken-fried steak. Caro had tasted that lumpy white gravy all night. At least there hadn't been some eligible pseudo-bachelor waiting at the impeccably-set table.

"Hey there, yourself." Caro used her foot to push out the other chair at her small table. "Sit, Pixie."

Jessie rested her hands on the back of the empty chair. "I will. Just let me grab one of what you're having. It smells really good."

"Caramel with a dash of salt, Jessie." Caro lifted her cup in salute. "Unexpected and delicious."

"Hmm, like somebody else I know."

Caro stared at her as she went up to the counter and gave her order to Becky's brother Tom. He quickly made her drink and Jessie rejoined Caro. She took the lid off of her cup and closed her eyes as she breathed in.

"Are you going to make love to that coffee?" Caro asked. "Or explain that cryptic statement you just made?"

Jessie took a delicate sip and sighed before opening her

eyes. "I was just speaking with the latest hot guy to fall into our midst."

Caro's cheeks went warm but she raised her brows. "Oh? Who?"

"Eli Graham, Caro." Jessie snorted. "As if you didn't know."

"So he's…what did you call him? Unexpected and delicious?"

"You tell me."

Caro fiddled with the corrugated cardboard sleeve wrapped around her cup. "Tell you what, exactly?"

"Tell me what's going on between the two of you?"

Caro stilled. Jeez, had someone seen them out by the lake, making out like their ship was sinking?

"Between us?" Oh, she was started to sound like an imbecile.

Jessie leaned closer. "I know you went out with him on Sunday."

Caro peeled away some of the cardboard sleeve, saying a silent prayer that Jessie wasn't talking about their dockside dalliance.

"Yes, I did. We went to Old Town Village, although you

probably know that already."

Jessie beamed and nodded her head. "I do. So tell me what's up with you two?"

"Nothing."

"Are you dating?"

"We went out on a date, but I'm not sure if we're actually dating."

"You shared a pizza at the tavern Monday night."

Caro splayed her hands on the table, staring her friend down over their coffee cups. "What, are you having me followed?"

Jessie reached out and covered one of her hands. "No. But you know as well as I do just how clear the glass is in this particular fishbowl."

"True." Caro straightened in her chair. "There's something between us, but who knows what? We're friends, sort of. I guess."

"Gee, what a lovely lukewarm sentiment."

"Jessie, you know me."

"I do."

"You know I don't play, but I don't have guy friends, either."

"Except for Eli."

She shrugged. "Apparently."

"Are you going out with him tonight?"

"I don't know. I don't think so."

"Do you want to?"

Caro managed a smile. "That's the question, isn't it?"

Jessie pushed aside her coffee cup and folded her hands. "I've known you for a year and a half, and I've never really seen you date."

"I've gone out a couple of times. With a couple of guys."

"And that's it?"

"I guess."

"Like I said, I've known you for some time now. You always seem content, or at least very grounded. This conversation about Eli, though? You seem really confused, Caro."

Caro grew quiet as she mulled over Jessie's words. "I guess I am. I really like him. Who wouldn't? He's fun."

"Yes, but there's something else beneath the surface. I got that vibe last spring when I toured him and the other Chapman guy. Now that I've been working with him for a few days? I see it more and more."

"What are you saying, Jessie?"

"Aren't you curious to see just what's beneath that yummy blond exterior?"

"Yummy?"

"I can say he's yummy. I'm married very happily to my own yummy blond guy."

Caro smiled a little. "So I should just take things as they come and worry about it later, is that what you're saying?"

Jessie held up her hands. "Hey, I was totally clueless when it came to Noah, Caro. I didn't even realize I loved him."

"Your story is nothing like mine."

"Maybe. Maybe not." Jessie's eyes darkened a little and her lips thinned. "We need to sit down and have a heart-to-heart. And soon."

"Now who has something else beneath the surface?" Caro teased.

Jessie's expression turned serious. "I think we all have things we're hiding, don't we?"

Caro's belly clenched as she recalled her own sad secret. "Maybe."

"One night you and I, Caro. We'll get a big bottle of wine, maybe head out to the tent-cabin and have that conversation."

"I'll consider it."

Jessie stood and placed the lid back on top of her coffee. "Max has soccer practice in about an hour. I'm grabbing some sandwiches at the market to bring to the field."

"Sounds like fun."

Jessie's smile was back, as was the light in her big brown eyes. "It is! I love being a mom."

Caro's breath stilled. She nodded mutely as Jessie left. Jessie was a mom, or at least a stepmom. Noah's little boy was six years old and stayed with them in Cypress about half of the time. Caro had a front seat, along with the rest of Cypress, and had watched as Jessie had resisted falling for Noah. She knew her friend would have a hard time putting the reason into words.

Something had happened to Jessie to make her hold herself back from that relationship. Something she was ultimately able to work through apparently, because now she was one of the happiest people Caro knew.

Eli was so tempting. Light and teasing and so good for her, at least as far as her social life was concerned. He wouldn't be the guy to push for more. Of that, she was reasonably sure. He'd said as much, hadn't he?

The trouble was, what if he did? Would she push right

back? Would she push him away or risk revealing her secrets, her hopes and dreams, to find out what they could have together?

She sipped her lukewarm coffee without tasting it as she wondered for a brief second just how happy she could really be. Someday.

Chapter 9

Caro woke on Thursday morning and stretched on her bed in her apartment, staring up at the plaster swirls in the ceiling above. She'd almost called Eli last night, after she'd gotten home at last. Her conversation with Jessie had stirred things up inside of her, but that could be due to the anniversary she'd acknowledged Monday afternoon.

She picked up her phone right as the alarm buzzed. Four o'clock. She smiled as she thought about Jane's comment. Oh dark thirty. Some mornings it felt like that.

"Another day, another dollar," she murmured as she began her day.

When she got to the bakery she found Jane inside already.

"Morning, boss!" she called over the sound of whirring mixers.

"Morning, Jane." Caro donned her big apron and got to work.

The morning flew by and by the time three o'clock rolled around she stopped long enough to take a breath.

"Wow, busy day," Jane observed. "Maybe we can use another kid during the week?"

"Expand our workforce?" Caro grinned. "Maybe."

Jane sipped her coffee from the shop next door. "You know, Tom said he'd like to learn how to bake."

"Seriously?"

"Yep. Said he's tired of just handing out plastic-wrapped biscotti."

"Biscotti." An idea came to Caro and she smiled.

Jane chuckled. "What are you thinking?"

"How about a pumpkin walnut biscotti for the Fall Fest?"

"That would give us almost two weeks to perfect it."

"And Sweet Escape serves nothing that isn't perfect," Caro said with a grin.

Jane got that familiar thoughtful expression and slipped on the glasses she kept on a chain around her neck. "Let me see."

As she thumbed through their box of recipes, Caro hid her smile. Of course they kept their recipes on the computer, but Jane always said she preferred the recipe cards in the funky green box. The little pink lady bug in the corner of the lid seemed to like the attention, too.

"We did something for the holidays last year…" Jane began.

Caro snapped her fingers. "Yes! The peppermint almond biscotti, drizzled with dark chocolate. Oh, that was good."

"And popular. If we really ramp up the cinnamon, nutmeg and cloves, leave out the peppermint of course, and sub chopped walnuts for the almond, maybe."

"And switch out the dark chocolate for white?" Caro added.

Jane gave a firm nod. "We just might have something there. It'll take a little experimentation."

"Which you know we can't stand, right?" Caro teased.

Jane smiled. "Okay, boss. We'll hit this tomorrow."

"Sounds great. Thanks, Jane."

They both left out the back door. As she watched Jane peddle off for home, she was once again seized by the distinct urge to avoid going to her own. Walking around the building, she stood and stared at the Fitness Center across the street. Pulling out her phone, she thumbed through the center's app and brought up the schedule of classes. There was a Yoga class starting at four thirty. Tapping to confirm attendance, she slipped the phone back in her pocket and returned to her car.

She always kept workout stuff in a bag in the little trunk, or at least workout clothes and a yoga mat. She wouldn't need her favorite running shoes or the super-supportive sports bra she liked to use when she ran. Nope. Just her mat and easy-peasy, comfy clothes to stretch or bend. And breathe.

Shouldering her bag and tucking her mat under her arm, she shut the trunk and hurried over to the Fitness Center. She hadn't practiced yoga in almost a week, and she'd missed it. She didn't even care if today's class was strengthening, relaxing or energizing. It could be general stretching or Vinyasa or Ashtanga. She just knew that it would feel good to focus on her breathing, which she'd often heard was what yoga was truly about. Breathing with some stretches and poses around it.

An hour later, after stretching and breathing and tightening her core, she felt like she had more space inside of her. Space to move and breathe, and some of her sadness receded to the back of her mind. There had been three other women attending the class whom she recognized enough to nod hello, and her favorite yogi had led the practice. On her mat, an island to herself as she'd followed the older woman's instructions, she'd found a little bit of clarity.

She thanked the instructor, wished the others in the class a good night, and walked out into the hallway. And right smack into Eli.

"Caro, hi." His smile was wide and bright. "What are you doing here?"

She patted the mat rolled up under her arm. "I'm done, actually. Yoga."

"I'm hitting the weight machines."

She ran her gaze over him. He looked really good in his workout clothes. He wore a sleeveless T-shirt in a dove gray and a pair of loose shorts in shiny navy blue. His legs looked strong but his arms looked even better.

"You work out with weights?" she asked, unable to think of anything more clever to say.

"A couple of times a week, yeah." His gaze took her in head to toe, and she felt a shiver that had nothing to do with the overactive A/C in the Fitness Center. "You?"

"Nope. I run and do yoga. Sometimes grab a Zumba class."

He brushed his golden waves back off his forehead and nodded. "I run, too. And swim. Yoga and Zumba? Not so much."

"Mmm hmm."

"So what are you up to later?"

She might have said something in answer but she wasn't sure. She tried to follow what he was saying but he looked so good. Dragging her naughty eyes up over his sculpted muscles, she looked him in the face. That was a mistake. His eyes held a tenderness along with that glint of sensuality she'd seen a couple of times by now. She completely lost her train of thought.

"Hmm?" She tried again. "What?"

He laughed, a secret, low rumble that made her tingle. Oh, she'd made space in her yoga class, all right. Space for wicked thoughts and desires that, at the moment, felt just right.

"I'd ask where your mind went Cupcake, but I'm pretty sure I can guess."

She licked her lips. "Oh, you can?"

He nodded as he reached for her. He just held her hand, gently stroking his thumb over the back of it. Yet her body heated and her breasts tingled. Oh, she'd made some space all right.

"Your mind went to that swing out by the lake," he said.

The swing. The lake. She swallowed a moan. *The kiss.*

Some of the things Jessie had said yesterday whispered in her ear once more. Maybe she should get to know Eli a little bit better. Learn what was beneath his sunny exterior. Right now that sounded like a fantastic idea. She took a breath and jumped right in.

"How about getting together after your workout?" she asked.

***

Eli stared at her for a beat, and then nodded. "That sounds really good to me, Cupcake."

Her blue-green eyes sparkled up at him. "What should we do, Graham Cracker?"

She placed a delicate hand in the center of his chest, not stroking, not moving, just resting it there. His heart pounded and his body reacted. Really glad for his loose shorts, he covered her hand with his.

"How about coming to my townhouse?"

She lifted her hand away from him as she blinked in obvious confusion. "Your what?"

"My townhouse."

Her brows knit. "You moved?"

"Not yet, but I signed the lease this afternoon. I have the keys."

A smile curved her full lips, and he was seized with the desire to kiss her crazy right here in the hallway. The fact that she wore some sexy-as-hell tight workout clothes wasn't helping him at the moment. Her breasts were caressed in Lycra and her bared belly was smooth and strong looking.

"You have the keys," she said.

He gave her a slow nod. "No furniture yet, but I can rough it if you can."

She laughed, a light sound he hadn't heard from her since they'd been up high on that Ferris wheel. "I hear a dare in there, Eli."

"Maybe." He winked, knowing he was turning on the charm. When her pretty eyes widened he knew he had her. Well, not completely. For dinner, at least.

"So where is this new place of yours?"

"Just a few doors down from Jessie and Noah Brady," he said. "The other end unit in that row."

"Oh, I'm glad you took it. That one's been empty for months now."

"That's what I'd heard. So, come by around seven?"

She nodded. "Do you want me to bring anything?"

He smiled. "I don't have anything yet, Cupcake. Bring whatever you like, as long as your sweet little self comes with it."

She shook her head at his ridiculous come-on line but her eyes danced. "Okay. I guess the electricity is on, or do you need candles?"

He just arched his brows and she slapped him right in the

center of his chest. This time she let her hand drift down over his abs before pulling away from him.

"The electricity is on," he said.

She nodded. "Go work out. I'm going home to shower and I'll meet you at your new house at seven."

He held in a fist pump, managing to simply nod as she walked away from him. Her ass looked amazing in those super-tight yoga pants. Sucking in a breath in an effort to cool his jets, he turned away and headed into the weight room.

After forty-five minutes he was ready to give it a rest. His muscles were humming and sweat streamed off of him and, while he'd initially anticipated working out for an hour or so, he now had a date tonight.

Nodding to another guy coming into the weight room as he exited, he headed for the men's locker room to shower and change into the cargo shorts and a T-shirt he'd shoved in his bag this morning. He'd left his SUV at the Sales Center, but as he walked back he passed it and went into the town market. It was nearly empty when he walked inside, and a glance at the posted business hours showed him the reason. They were only open for twenty minutes longer. He went to the case holding prepared foods and grabbed up a couple of sandwiches. He crossed to the chips and snacks aisle and a display at the front of the store caught his eye.

Bales of hay and pumpkins sprinkled with fake fall leaves were artfully arranged, along with pumpkin-spice donuts and other fall-flavored products placed on and around it. There was a wicker basket on display too, holding a couple of wine bottles, some plastic plates and utensils, and a blue and green plaid blanket.

"Excuse me?" He went up to the tall, skinny kid working the counter. "I know you're closing in a little while, but could I get one of those blankets? And a basket, too."

The kid stared at him through his round glasses. "What?"

"The display? Over by the door?"

"Oh, yeah. They were putting that up earlier but I haven't seen it."

"So?"

"We don't sell those things," the kid said. "At least I don't think we do."

"Oh, let the boy have his basket and blanket, Jordy," a portly guy said with a smile.

"Okay, Dad."

The kid rushed out from behind the counter to grab the

things for Eli.

"Thanks." Eli held out his hand to the guy, who was just as tall as his son. "Eli Graham."

They shook hands. "Pete Becker."

"Are you sure I can take your display?"

The man grinned. "I think it proves that display is a pretty good advertisement, huh? I can get some more baskets and blankets from the sporting goods store in the square." He winked. "Think I can get away with a little mark-up?"

Eli smiled. This guy had the sales touch. "I don't see why not."

"For you, Mr. Graham?" He winked again. "I'll give it to you at cost."

Eli laughed as the kid came back to the counter with the basket and blanket. "Sounds good. Now how about recommending a wine to go with these sandwiches?"

Pete nodded and walked him over to the upended crates holding the wine selection. By the time Eli checked out, he had everything for a picnic supper with Caro.

Previously he hadn't been in the market for any longer than it took to grab a cold drink out of the coolers near the entrance, but it looked like they carried just about everything. A glance told him the prices seemed reasonable, considering the convenience to residents and visitors. He'd make sure to mention the place on his next tour.

He got to the townhouse with five minutes to spare. The basket, and everything he'd bought for tonight, fit under his arm as he unlocked his new place. The key stuck for a second and then the clicked the lock open. He swung the door inward and stepped inside. The A/C was running, he knew you never turned off the air in a property down here unless you wanted mold or worse, but it wasn't as cool as he'd like. He walked past a small office to the left and on through to the big kitchen to set the basket on the light granite counter. The kitchen's dark wood cabinets looked a little dusty and the place was dim. The fridge was running, so he stowed the sandwiches and six-pack of beer he'd bought. The bottle of wine, he set on the counter. He checked the tap and the water was on. Pretty good pressure, too.

Making a mental note to pick up cleaning supplies for this weekend, he went through the place turning the lights on. A ceiling fan turned lazily above the great room and the wide-plank floors looked to be in pretty good condition. A stone fireplace was opposite the tall counter in the kitchen, and there was an empty dining area with a glass and wire fixture hanging over it.

There was a half bath tucked under the stairs at the back of the great room. Toilet flushed, faucet ran, so he went up the polished wood stairs. There he found two good-sized bedrooms, a guest bath and double doors that had to lead to the master suite. He pushed them open and he wasn't disappointed. The room was huge with a vaulted ceiling. A wall of windows showed the views of golf course and conservation areas. The windows were bare except for the same plantation shutters on the ones downstairs. He peeked into the big bathroom set beside a walk-in closet and was further impressed with the tile work and fixtures. He checked the water here as well, even the dual heads in the massive shower. He suddenly pictured soaping up the delectable Caro Richmond in that shower. Stretching her out on that built-in bench seat and spreading suds all over her toned and curvy body.

The doorbell rang from downstairs, and he grinned. It was the fantasy herself. He descended the stairs and went to the front door. He pulled it open and found her standing there, holding a square pan covered in aluminum foil. She wore jeans and a soft-looking shirt in light blue. Her hair was down, and shone beneath the porch light overhead.

"Come in, Cupcake." He stepped back to let her in. "You look fantastic. Not that I didn't like the way you looked in your yoga clothes."

"Thanks." She turned a little pink but she smiled at him and held up the pan. "I brought a treat."

"Yeah, you did."

Her laugh was easy and rolled over him in the best way. "So come on, Graham Cracker. Show me your new place."

He couldn't keep the grin off of his face if he tried. And if he got his wish, he'd put more than a smile on her pretty face.

Chapter 10

Caro looked around the stark emptiness of Eli's new place. It was a mirror-image of Jessie and Noah's place, but done in darker woods for the floors and cabinets. She set the still-warm, foil-covered pan of caramel brownies on the tall counter next to a big wicker basket. She'd made them in her apartment when she'd gotten home from the Fitness Center. It had done her good to keep herself occupied as she'd anticipated taking this next step with Eli.

"What do you think?" he asked.

"I like it." She smiled. "Very minimalist."

"Funny. Do you want to see upstairs?"

"I think we should save something for the next time I'm over."

"The next time, huh?"

She shrugged. "You know. Next time. When you have furniture?"

"And a bed upstairs?"

She held up a hand. "Don't get ahead of yourself, Eli. So what's for dinner?"

"Sandwiches from the market, if that's okay."

"That's great." She walked around the counter and placed

her hands on her hips. "Where are we eating?"

He grabbed a pretty blanket done in a blue and green plaid out of the basket and crossed to the front of the fireplace. "We're having a picnic, Caro." After spreading the blanket on the wood floor he peered into the fireplace. "Looks like the gas is turned on."

"It's a little warm for a fire," she said.

"Gives us something to look forward to, then. It does get cold down here, doesn't it? Sometime?"

"We get a few cold snaps, but it's not like you're used to. Brisk and chilly in the late autumn and actually cold in January."

"Florida cold?" He smirked. "What's that, like fifty degrees?"

"Just wait. Even you, with your thick Northern blood, will need a sweater then."

He went back to the kitchen and picked up the basket. "Grab the wine, would you?"

She did and joined him as he set the basket on the blanket. He unpacked plates, napkins, flatware, and two wine glasses as she opened the wine. He took the bottle from her and poured. Handing her one glass, he held the other up. "To my new place."

She toasted him. "To home."

A strange expression crossed his face, gone in the next second. He'd almost looked sad, but that was something that seemed so out of place with him she must have been mistaken. He blinked, and that familiar grin tugged at his lips. She took a sip as he did, and then he jumped up to grab their dinner out of the fridge.

"I bought a couple of different kinds, so take your pick."

She set her glass down and looked through the wrapped sandwiches. They were all big and looked to be double-stuffed with meat and cheese. She settled on a turkey with Colby on Italian bread, cutting it in half and wrapping the rest up to leave for him. As they began their picnic dinner, she looked around the great room.

"This really is a nice place, Eli." She dug into a little bag of baked sweet potato chips and crunched for a minute. "Where do you plan on going for furniture?"

"Already found a site online. Point and click, baby."

"Sounds so personal. Don't you want to try it out before you buy it?"

He set his sandwich down and leveled a hot look at her. "If you're asking about my bed, yeah. That's something I'm going to try out in person before making a purchase."

She felt a flush all over her body, like she had when he'd eyed her in her yoga clothes. "I wasn't asking. You should know that there are at least twenty mattress stores in St. Cloud. I don't know why, but it seems that every time a new storefront opens it's another mattress store."

"Sounds like a sleepy little town. I haven't really been anywhere but the sports bar."

"It's got the usual big box stores, fast food places and auto repair shops. It's the closest city to Cypress, so if you need anything the market or sporting goods store doesn't have that's your place."

"I like the little market. Met Pete and his son today, actually. He sold me this basket and blanket right out of their fall display."

She laughed lightly. "Yes, Pete will do anything to make a sale. His prices aren't too crazy, either."

He nodded and drank his wine, his eyes on her. Once again she got that feeling that there was more to him than the easygoing charmer. She couldn't guess what he was thinking at the moment. When he licked his lips, she sure knew what she was thinking.

She drained her wine and set her empty glass and plate to

the side. "This is nice. Sitting here and having a picnic. Thanks for inviting me."

"I promise I'll cook for you next time if you give me that treat you brought."

She got up and went to the kitchen. Bringing the square pan back to the blanket, she rifled through the utensils in the basket and came up with a knife and fork.

He eyed the pan. "What did you make, Caro?"

"Brownies."

His brows rose. "The s'mores ones?"

She shook her head. "Caramel."

He rolled his eyes and groaned. "You're killing me, Cupcake."

She beamed a smile at him as she peeled off the foil and began to cut into the crisp and chewy top of the brownies. Before she could serve them he went at the pan with a fork.

"Eli!"

"I couldn't wait," he said around a mouthful of food. "Mmm, my God."

She took a bite right from the pan too. It tasted pretty good to her, if not perfect. "I didn't have time to make my own caramel so I melted the kind you dip apples in."

"It's fantastic." He scooped another big bite. "Man."

She sat back and watched as he savored her dessert. His strong throat worked as a look of bliss crossed his face. Her body began to tingle and her lips parted as she hungered for a taste of him right now.

"I'm glad you like it," she managed to say.

He must have caught something in her tone of voice, because his eyes opened and pinned her with their intensity. "Caro."

Oh, the way he said her name. Low and a little rough.

"What?" she breathed.

He set his fork down and cleared the blanket with a careful sweep of his hands. "Come here."

She couldn't stop herself if she wanted to. Tucking her head into the crook of his neck, she breathed him in. He smelled so good. Fresh and hot. Her tongue flicked out to taste his skin and he growled.

Cupping her face, he stared into her eyes and her pulse raced. Parting her lips, she welcomed his kiss when it came. This kiss was hot. Wet. Different from their kiss on the Ferris wheel. Deeper than the time out by the lake. When he eased her down on the blanket she went willingly. His big body felt so good covering hers and she nearly purred as she rubbed against him.

He tunneled his hands through her hair and nuzzled her neck. "You're killing me, you know that?"

He'd said that before, about the brownies. The man had appetites, and she loved knowing that he craved her right now.

"Touch me, Eli."

He lifted his head and kissed her again, pinning her down in the best way as he stroked her beneath her shirt. He pushed the fabric up and she held up her arms so he could take it off of her. His face was between her breasts now, his tongue stroking over her skin as he ran his thumbs over her nipples.

"That feels so good," she sighed.

"You smell so sweet." He teethed one nipple and she cried out. "Sweet Cupcake."

The nickname was silly but she loved hearing it from him. His voice was rough and his touch insistent as he removed her bra. Easing up on his hands, he stared at her.

"You have the prettiest tits." He licked her other nipple and her heart began to pound. "I could kiss them all night."

She held his head with one hand, then tugged him up to kiss her again. Cradling his hips, she felt the long hard length of him. She wasn't ready for that tonight, but she needed something.

Pushing him up slightly, she worked her hands under his shirt and he pulled it over his head to toss it on the floor with hers. She gaped at him. He was beautiful. Sculpted and strong and his chest was dusted with just a bit of golden hair that darkened as it led downward below his navel. She saw the hint of those sexy indents on his pelvis and she wanted to touch him all over. She gave in, palming his muscles as she felt the heat and strength of him.

He woke something in her she'd never felt before. Not with Brad and not with the couple of guys since the accident. Lust, yes. But there was something else. He was a good time. Of that she was absolutely sure. And tonight? She might not end up sleeping with him but she was going to have a good time.

***

Eli sensed a change in Caro, and her movements became more focused. On his dick, actually. She took her busy hands from his chest and reached down to cup him through his shorts. He let out a moan. He'd never been this hard, and all they'd done was a little bit of petting.

"You're driving me crazy, baby." He unbuttoned her jeans and slipped a finger just a little bit down her pants. "Am I making you wet?"

"Y-yes."

He wanted to do everything at once. Kiss her beautiful breasts all night. Stroke her until she came. Lick her until she cried his name. That was a lot to expect tonight but he wanted to give her a taste of what she made him feel just by being in his arms.

He unzipped her jeans and eased two fingers into her. She was hot. Wet. Her moans were as sweet as she was as she arched against him. He wasn't sure how she'd done it but his shorts were down past his ass and she was stroking him. It would be so easy to slip inside of her. To ride her until they were both satisfied. He held himself back, though he wasn't sure why at this very second.

Closing his eyes, he began to pump into her hand. It was awkward and perfect and he never wanted her to stop touching him. Holding himself up, he stared down at where she now had both hands on him. His gaze flicked to her face and he saw she was staring up at him. Her eyes were dark blue now, nearly the blue of the blanket beneath her.

"Eli," she whispered.

It was suddenly too much and he came hard against her

bare belly. He was still shaking when he reached for a stack of napkins and wiped her clean. In the next second he pulled off her jeans, taking her panties with them. Cupping her perfect ass, he held her up and licked her.

"Oh!"

Her fingers cradled his head again, as she had when he'd kissed her breasts. She was sweet here, too. Straining toward him, she spread her legs further and he licked and nibbled until she was coming as hard as he had. He found her clit and sucked it, and her moans echoed off the high ceilings of the empty room.

She was sobbing now, and he gentled as he eased away from her. Eyes closed and breathing hard through parted lips, she was obviously spent and he couldn't help but grin as he tucked himself back into his pants.

"You're sweet all over, Cupcake."

She took in deep breath and slowly let it out, fluttering her eyes open to gaze up at him. "That was amazing."

"Hey, I had to do something to repay you for those brownies."

She laughed at that and he helped her sit up. "What time is it?"

"No idea." He fished around in his pocket and found his phone. "Almost nine."

She sighed and tucked her legs against her chest. "By the way, why am I naked and you still have almost all of your clothes on?"

"My clothes had easier access."

She pushed at him as she shook her head. "You're bad."

"Nah, I'm good. Which I think I just proved."

She grabbed up her hair and twisted it over her shoulder like he'd seen her do before. "Thank God this place is soundproof."

"How do you know that?"

She winked at him, adorable and sexy at the same time. "Jessie told me. She knows the specs on just about everything in Cypress."

"I'm glad." He stood and handed her clothes, unable to look away as she covered all of that delectable flesh even as he knew he should. "I wouldn't want my neighbors complaining before I even officially move in."

Dressed again, she stood and stretched. Rubbing her perfect ass, she groaned. "I think you need furniture, Eli."

"Come help me pick out a bed?"

She held up a hand. "You don't need my help. You're a big boy."

"Which I also proved tonight."

She stared at him for a second, and then smiled. "This was fun. Thanks again."

"Thanks for the brownies and the hand job."

She snorted out a laugh and then covered her mouth. "I have to get up early in the morning. Jane and I are trying out a new recipe for the Fall Festival."

"Just make those brownies, Caro. Although they weren't the tastiest thing I had tonight."

Rolling her eyes as she blushed, she covered the brownies with the foil. "I'll leave these here with you, if you can stand it."

"Are you kidding? I just may eat the rest of them before your taillights disappear."

He walked her to the front door, and then drew her close and kissed her. He let his tongue move slowly through her mouth as he splayed one hand on her back and the other on one ass cheek. Lifting away from her at last, he nipped at her bottom lip. "See you tomorrow?"

"You know where I'll be."

He nodded and kissed her again because he just couldn't

help himself. She left and he ran a hand through his hair. That wasn't what he'd expected tonight. Making out, sure. Maybe it was just getting a little something-something, but it felt like more. She was sweet. He hadn't been exaggerating. Her touch was like magic on him, and he'd been more than thrilled to return the favor.

She seemed to like him, but then again most people did. That was what he excelled at. Getting people to like him. Caro was different somehow. There was that sad story in her past, which she'd talked a little bit about out at the lake. He wasn't the guy to push for more disclosure. He kept his own sad story locked away behind smiles and charm.

She was a keeper, though. That was clear, from the friends she had here to the family that supported her. She was a keeper and he was a shiny toy that got tossed away when it was finished being played with.

"That's the way it is," he told himself as he cleaned and straightened his new place. "Never gonna change, my man."

Even if he wanted it to? Even if he wanted to see what having a real relationship was like? It didn't matter.

That was one deal he had no idea how to close.

Chapter 11

Oh dark thirty on Friday morning, or four thirty actually, Caro was humming as she sampled a tiny taste of the mixture of spices in the small glass bowl. Adding another teaspoon of nutmeg, she jotted it down on the recipe card and stirred.

"What has you so happy this morning?" Jane asked as she switched out baked cupcakes for ready-to-bake in the big oven.

Caro felt her cheeks warm but she kept her eyes on the swirl of brown spices. "Just breathing in the scent of fall in a bowl, Jane."

Jane went quiet and Caro hesitantly brought her eyes up to hers. The older woman was shaking her head as she closed the oven door. "I'm not buying it. You were mopey at the beginning of the week and now?"

"Now I'm not mopey?" Caro offered.

"You're downright chipper. Something happened."

Yeah, it did. "I don't know what you're talking about."

Jane snorted as she lifted the cupcakes onto a rack to cool. "I know you, Caro. I've seen you in the wee hours of the morning when nothing can hide."

"You don't know everything about me." Caro sprinkled the spice mixture into the biscotti dough she'd already prepped.

153

"Can't a girl have secrets?"

Jane laughed now. "A girl can try, but I'm thinking something happened with that blond god we all know and lust after."

Caro smiled and slipped on a pair of plastic prep gloves. "He's not a god, but he's sure close."

Jane's mouth dropped open. "You... You and Eli... Something happened."

Caro turned the spiced dough onto the wide wooden board as she shook her head. "As you've said, you're old enough to be his mother. You can't possibly want to hear just what happened last night, do you?"

Jane clasped her hands together, the smile wreathing her face making her look closer to twenty than fifty. "Did you let your fingers do the walking?"

Caro's hands stilled on the dough. "How could you possibly know that?"

Jane lifted her chin at the pile of dough. "Just look."

Caro saw that she'd smoothed the dough into a long, thick cylinder and shook her head. "You have a dirty mind, Jane. I'm making biscotti."

"Maybe that's a good thing. That looks pretty darn big to

me." Jane opened her mouth to say something else that would probably have Caro confessing to what else had happened last night when the oven timer went off. "This isn't over."

Caro gave a noncommittal shrug and returned her focus to the completely-innocent biscotti dough. Kneading it thoroughly to mix in all the spices, she let her mind drift back to the incredible way Eli had made her feel. She'd teased him, which always seemed to get him to say the cheesiest or most outrageous lines. The banter had been absent as they'd begun to tease each other in an entirely different way. Oh, she'd never been so bold before but she'd had to get her hands on him.

She began to add the chopped walnuts to the dough, and was soon humming again as she mixed everything together. The dough would be baked twice, which would give it its crispiness. The spices had to stand up to it, and this first batch would be just the beginning. She formed a long loaf about five inches wide on a baking sheet lined with parchment and slid it into the waiting oven. She'd have to keep an eye on it, since in addition to the mixture of spices it had a healthy dose of canned pumpkin.

Discarding her gloves, she grabbed up the torch and crossed to the s'mores brownies that were nearly finished.

"It's seven," Jane chirped.

Caro glanced at the antique-looking oversized clock hanging in the dining area and nodded. "Let's start the madness."

It was just something to say, as she'd yet to open the doors this early to a hoard of customers. The sun was up, more or less, and she unlocked the door and pulled it open just to hear the chime. The silly little riff always lifted her spirits. She'd told Eli she'd needed fun when she'd first opened the bakery and, after last night? Apparently she still did.

She and Jane switched off helping with customers and finishing up the day's offerings. Once the loaf of biscotti dough had baked the first time, she'd let it cool a little and now sliced it on the diagonal in even pieces to bake again. The baked dough was a lovely shade of tan with a touch of orange from the pumpkin, and sprinkled throughout with browns of different colors from the spices and walnuts. She arranged the slices on a fresh piece of parchment and slipped them into the oven for their second go-around. They would only take a few minutes to crisp up nice and toasty.

"Back in the oven, Jane," she called.

"I'll watch them," Jane answered.

"Something smells so good!" a woman said from out in the

shop.

Caro stepped out of the kitchen to find Claire Chapman standing in the middle of the dining area, holding a cup of coffee from next door. Claire, the CPA and controller of Cypress, was due to have her much-anticipated baby next month but other than her round belly she looked trim. Her long strawberry blond waves were held back with a wide headband and her face was nearly free of makeup. She was a natural beauty, and her freckles made her blue eyes sparkle. Not to mention she wore a thin cardigan in her trademark color of poppy orange.

"Claire Chapman, darkening my doorstep?" Caro teased.

"Hi, Caro." Claire closed her eyes and lifted her nose in the air before facing her again. "Oh, what is that delicious smell?"

"Wouldn't you like to know?"

Claire was one of the best home bakers Caro had ever met, and they'd had a friendly rivalry over whose treats were the best.

"No, Caro." Claire beamed a smile at her. "You know I love everything you make."

"You love everything you can't make yourself."

"Too true." She rested a hand on her belly and sighed. "Besides, soon I'll be too busy to bake much of anything."

Caro felt a stab of want that took her breath away. She

157

hadn't thought very often about the baby she'd lost other than the awful anniversary each year, and now here she was envying what Claire would soon have.

"So what can I get you this morning?" Caro asked, hoping to hide her strange mood behind her usual courtesy.

"I need my fall fix, Caro." She held up the cup in her hand. "A pumpkin spice latte loses something when it's made with decaf."

Caro shivered. "Ooh, decaf. I feel for you. Why bother, right?"

"Right. So why don't you tell me what you're making that I smell? You know about pregnant women, right? We develop a heightened sense of smell."

"The super-smeller. Yep. Tammy used to come floating in here all the time before she had Raffaella."

Claire nodded. "Yep. Believe me, it's not all sweets and flowers. The super-smeller is no treat when Jake comes home from the Adventure Trails."

Caro laughed. Jake designed and developed the trails up and across the main lakeshore, and they were popular with corporate retreats looking for mild thrills and serious athletes looking to run triathlons. Jake's sister Cassie worked there too, with the kids' program. Nick, Rick Chapman's little boy, served as their official test-marketer and research guy.

"I could imagine. I haven't been on the climbing walls in weeks. It's just too hot."

"I'm with you." She took a sip of her drink and shook her head. "Just not the same. Now what are you making?"

"You're tenacious, you know that?"

"And you're trying to distract me."

Caro shrugged. "Jane and I are working on a new treat for the Fall Festival. Very hush-hush."

"I'm the sole of discretion, Caro."

"Maybe, but this isn't about Cypress's financial bottom line."

Claire's expression grew serious. "No, but it is about yours."

Caro nodded. "Okay. Pumpkin Walnut Spice biscotti."

Claire's eyes went round. "Oh my God, I think the baby kicked just hearing you say that."

Caro smiled. "Let me see if I have one cooled and ready."

Claire nodded, her eyes bright. "Yes, please!"

Jane had set the tray of toasted cookies aside, and Caro picked one up with a small sheet of waxed paper. She brought it out to Claire and handed it to her.

"Now, this is just preliminary. Once we get the dough right, we'll drizzle them with white chocolate."

Claire took a bite and closed her eyes. "Oh, my God," she mumbled with a mouth full of cookie. "This is so good."

Caro felt a flush of pride like she always did when someone praised her work. "Thanks. Um, what do you think about the spices?"

"Well." Claire took another bite and chewed before answering. "My sense of taste is off because of this little one, but I think its plenty spicy. I love the combination, and the pumpkin gives it a chewiness you don't often find in biscotti."

Caro nodded. "Good! We'll probably ramp up the spices so the non-pregnant taste buds can get a shot."

"You haven't tried them yet?"

Caro shook her head. "They only just cooled."

Claire finished the cookie and held her hand over her heart. "Thanks for trusting me, Caro. With the cookie, of course. But also with your work."

Caro's throat tightened. She might not have hung out with Claire, or Jessie for that matter, in a while due to their differing schedules but it was nice to know she had friends here in

Cypress. "No trouble trusting you."

"I should get to work, though. Mid-month numbers are due."

"Have at them. It was really nice to see you."

"Thanks. Good luck with the recipe and we have to get together soon." She rubbed her belly again. "Clock's ticking."

Caro nodded and shooed her out the door. She turned to find Jane holding a biscotti toward her and another in her own hand.

"What did Claire have to say about it?" Jane asked.

"She loved it, but I think I might have to adjust the spices since she has pregnancy taste buds."

She took the cookie from Jane and broke it in half. The walnuts and spices looked to be evenly distributed and the cookie smelled delicious. One bite and she knew her instincts were right.

Jane bit into hers and chewed. "The spices are nearly there, though. I'd add more clove, I think."

"We'll have to try again, and that's the fun of it right?"

"Damn right," Jane grinned.

***

Eli finished up his first solo tour and headed back into the

Sales Center. It was just three o'clock, and his eyes automatically strayed toward the bakery. He could write up his impressions of the couple he'd toured in a few minutes. He had to see Caro first.

The five-note chime welcomed him into the shop, which was empty of any other customers.

"Be right with you!" Caro called from the back.

"Sure thing," he answered.

She popped her head out from the kitchen. "Eli?" A smile curved her lips. "Just the man I wanted to see."

He blinked at her words. "Yeah?"

She brushed her hands over her apron and nodded. "Yes. I want you to taste something."

He arched a brow at her and her answering laugh made his belly clench. "Hmm. Interesting."

She waved a hand and ducked back into the kitchen. When she reemerged she held a cookie in her hand. A biscotti, actually.

"Here. Taste this."

He took the cookie and eyed it. It was a tan and orange color, and looked delicious. He sniffed it, and took a bite. Immediately his mouth watered as the spices mingled on his tongue. It was crunchy and chewy and just about perfect.

162

"Do you like it?" she asked, her eyes intent.

He swallowed and nodded. "Man, that's good. Pumpkin spice?"

She grinned. "Yep. What do you think of the spice blend?"

He took another bite and moaned softly. "I'm no baker, but I think it's damn near perfect."

"Told you!" An older woman stepped out of the kitchen with a smile. "We've got it, Caro."

"Definitely." He popped the last bit of cookie in his mouth and chewed before holding out his hand to her. "Jane, I take it?"

"Yep." She gave his hand a pump and released it. "Eli?"

"That's me." He faced Caro. "You've got this one, Cupcake."

She flushed with obvious pride, and little bit of embarrassment unless he missed his guess. "Thanks. Wait until we add the white chocolate."

He groaned. "You're going to kill it at the festival."

Caro did a cute little fist pump. "Yeah, we will!"

Jane was eyeing him and he wondered if she knew what he'd gotten up to with her boss. At least she didn't seem to be measuring him, like he'd felt when Lettie had checked him out.

"So when are you done?" he asked Caro as Jane went back

into the kitchen.

"We're getting ready to close, and then we have to finish cleaning up. You?"

"I'm done at five. Want to grab dinner?"

She placed her hands on her hips. "Eli, people will talk."

"In my experience, Cupcake? People will talk no matter what."

"That's just about what I told her," Jane added from the back.

"Quiet, you!" Caro called back. "Okay, dinner it is. Do you have furniture yet?"

"Ordered it today. It's being delivered tomorrow morning."

"Wow, that's fast."

"I'm leasing everything but the bed. Even a washer and dryer."

"You're leasing your furniture?"

"Sure. Why not?"

"I...I'm not sure." She fingered the tie of her apron. "Tomorrow, huh?"

"Yep. I plan to clean the whole place tomorrow and get all settled in. Maybe I'll have a fire."

"September in Florida, Eli."

He shrugged. "Yeah, it got pretty hot in there last night."

She slid him a smile. "I'll have to get you a housewarming gift."

He nearly choked as he pictured her wrapped up in a ribbon and nothing else. "I can think of something," he said in a low voice.

She clicked her tongue as she ushered him to the door and flipped over the cardboard sign to read Closed. He glanced toward the kitchen and saw they were relatively alone, and bent his head to kiss her. Their lips clung for a second, and he pulled back with a smile. She looked a little surprised by the gesture, and frankly so was he.

"See you later, Cupcake."

Opening the door, the cheerful chimes sounded again as he walked out. Those chimes were fun, she'd said. She'd needed some fun when she'd first opened. She'd said that, too. It had to have something to do with whatever had made her so sad out by the lake that day. He sure hoped she needed the kind of fun he liked having with her, because they were only getting started.

The afternoon went by pretty quickly, and he began to shut everything down.

"Nice job with that last tour, Eli."

165

He glanced up to find Jessie standing there. "Thanks, Jessie."

"And guess what happened with the family you toured on Wednesday?"

"What?"

"Noah just told me they're going forward with one of the spec homes in the green neighborhood."

"That's great." This would be his first sale based on his own tour and sales pitch. "Very nice."

Jessie nodded. "Noah said they couldn't say enough about the way you really made them see how happy their family could be in Cypress."

Eli gaped at her. "Seriously?"

"Yes, seriously." She blinked at him. "Why?"

"Honestly? I felt like I was talking out of my ass on that tour."

"Well, they must have sensed something about it because they also said you seemed like you really got the whole family thing."

Her cell phone rang and she went to go take her call. Eli sat back and tried to work his mind around what she'd told him. He must be better than even he thought he was, if he'd been able to make that family think he actually bought into the concept himself.

He scrubbed a hand over his face and finished clearing his desk in anticipation of another weekend off. He wouldn't think about the way he'd framed just how that family's life could be if they settled in Cypress Corners. He'd just recited what he'd read. What he'd heard Jessie and Bree and Oliver say on the tours he'd shadowed. He had no fucking clue about family himself.

Shoving aside the whole damn business, he closed up shop and thought about his upcoming dinner with Caro. A smile tugged his lips. Maybe he'd get her to help him pick out a bed.

Chapter 12

"So this is what it's like to finally get you into bed."

Eli's voice was low and rumbly, his lips very close to Caro's ear. Even though his words sent a tingle through her, she laughed and wriggled her toes.

"Finally? We've known each other for about a week, Eli."

"Still." He stretched his big frame and his feet nearly reached the bottom of the mattress. "It's hard to know if this bed is right for me. Who knows if you kick in your sleep? Hog the covers? Could be a big mistake."

They were side by side and fully dressed, on a memory foam king-sized mattress in the first store they'd come to in St. Cloud, staring up at the ceiling. The store was much like any other, with rows of undressed mattresses made of various foams and mattress-y things. Caro wasn't sure what all of it was, but this mattress they were sharing at the moment felt pretty comfortable. It was the sixth they'd tried out.

"Do you like *this* one?" she asked him.

Eli shrugged his shoulders and threw his arms wide, his hand just brushing the top of her head. "Hug me."

She turned her head to eye him. "Hug you?"

He grinned. "Trying to keep it G-rated, Cupcake."

"It's your mattress, Eli."

In answer to her counterpoint, he began to move up and down, holding his body taut and bowing back on every bounce. She glanced around and saw that several of the other customers in the store were starting to stare.

"You're treading into PG-13 territory, Graham Cracker."

He laughed and settled back down. "Still, you didn't seem to bounce at all. That's a good thing, right?"

"It sure is," said a salesman in khakis and a white oxford shirt standing a few beds away from them. "No transfer of motion."

Eli slid her a look and she could just guess what he was going to say next. He'd probably point out the kind of motion he'd like to transfer or something like that.

She sat up and covered his mouth with her fingers. "Don't even think about it."

He smiled beneath her fingers and then sat up too. She lowered her hand and he swung his legs over the side of the bed. "I like this one. The lady wouldn't hug me, but I can imagine how it would feel."

She shook her head. "Eli."

Grinning, he stood and reached into his pocket. "Let's do

this, my man."

The salesman nodded. "Great! When do you want us to deliver one of these Sleep Star Beauty kings?"

Eli stared at him, and then looked at the large hang tag. Caro stifled a laugh at the silly name and the incredulous expression on Eli's face.

"Tomorrow."

The guy hurried around to the sales counter and clicked on the keyboard as he stared at the computer screen. "You're in luck! We have it in stock right here in St. Cloud and can set it up for Saturday delivery!"

"Cool." Eli drew out his credit card and tapped it on the counter. "I'll need a platform for it."

"What type?"

"Something in a dark wood." Eli pointed to a bed an aisle over. "Nothing fancy."

The salesman clicked as he added the model to Eli's order. "Done."

"I'll need bedding and stuff, too."

The salesman brightened. "We're having our Labor Day sale right now, and we'll include a six-hundred count Egyptian cotton sheet set and coverlet, along with two king pillows."

"Labor Day?" Eli asked. "That was, like, two weeks ago."

"Yeah, the holidays get longer every year." The guy shrugged. "We have to do something to get us to Columbus Day."

Eli finished up his sale and he and Caro made their way back outside. "That was pretty easy."

"Easy? If you think so."

"How about the End Zone for dinner, Caro."

"Sounds good."

Eli drove them to the sports bar and she saw that the lot was getting pretty full. They were able to get a booth over on the dining side of the place, and the high wood backs made the spot feel very private. Almost intimate.

The perky ponytailed server from her last visit was back, and greeted Eli like she was meeting an old friend. She was a bit less enthusiastic in her address to Caro.

"What are you drinking?" she asked them.

"Pumpkin ale, please," Caro said.

"And a Bud for me." He looked at Caro. "Plate of hot wings, Cupcake?"

"Sure," Caro answered. "And the fish tacos."

"Make my dinner a burger. Medium rare," Eli said.

171

The server left them and Eli rested his folded arms on the table. "Is the food good here? You know, other than the wings?"

"It's okay. The fish tacos are surprisingly tasty."

The wings and beers soon arrived and they started what Caro was beginning to think of as their third date. There were all kinds of expectations on a third date. Sexual ones. Since she'd already gotten her hands on him, she anticipated that something more might happen sometime soon. He did just order a bed, after all.

"So you're going to be cleaning and setting up your place this weekend," she began.

"That's the plan. Sunday, though? I plan to spend that with my favorite baker."

She flushed a little. His flirting comments were always delivered with that clear, crystal gaze. "I'll look forward to seeing just what kind of home you'll set up with your point-and-click method."

"Hmm. Maybe you should show me your place as a point of reference?"

"No way, Eli. You set foot in my apartment and my mother will be setting a place for you at the family dinner table."

The surprise on his face was comical. "Why?"

Caro turned her glass on the tabletop as she chose her words. "She's been trying to fix me up."

He nodded. "Yeah, I remember now. Any new slug men on the horizon?"

"I hope not."

Eli drank from his bottle as he eyed her. "You know, I don't think I've ever been to a family dinner table."

"Seriously? You, blond god that you are, never dated a girl who wanted to take you home to mom?"

"Oh, they all wanted to take me home." His eyes sparkled in the low light of the bar. "Just not to their mom."

"Well, don't worry. I'll make sure my mother doesn't extend the invitation." She teased him now. "I'll run interference for you."

"Fair enough."

Their meals arrived and they chatted a little as they ate. By the time they were through, he wore a different expression on his face. He was looking down, and his brow was knit.

"Eli?"

He looked up and his expression cleared. "Sorry. I was thinking about what we might want to do on Sunday."

"I don't think that's what you were thinking about."

"All right. You got me. I was hoping that you would tell your mom to call off the hunt, so to speak."

Whoa. Did he want them to be exclusive? Heck, did she?

"Are you asking me to only date you?"

"I'll make you a deal, Cupcake. How about just you and me for now?"

"For now?"

"I don't know if this job will work out. Who knows if I'll be staying in Cypress?"

She was aware that he had an end date here. From what she'd learned of him so far, he always had an end date.

"Look, I get it," she began. "Your house is rented. Your furniture leased. It's like it's all a trial membership, or something."

"Maybe." There was a lot in that one word. Like maybe he wasn't completely okay with it but it was what it was.

"I do know I like being with you, Eli. The talking and the sexy stuff, too."

"What about your family?"

"What about them?"

"Don't they need to know what's going on in your life?"

"I'm twenty-seven, so no."

He wore that thoughtful expression again. "Still."

"Why? Does your family always need to know what's up with you?"

That odd look crossed his face again. "I don't have any family."

***

Eli saw the curiosity on Caro's face, and looked for the pity that usually came after he made this particular disclosure. Not that he'd told many women about this. He almost always managed to end whatever was going on between them before the subject of family even came up. One- or two-night stands don't usually ask about it.

"I didn't know that," she said.

He folded and unfolded one corner of his napkin over and over, his gaze on the table again. "Go ahead and ask."

She reached across the table and touched his hand, stilling him. "You don't have to tell me anything, Eli. It's none of my business."

He looked up and found her blue-green gaze direct. Open but not probing. "There's nothing to tell, really. I'm an orphan. Grew up in foster care."

He watched her swallow down his confession. Nodding,

she stroked his hand. "You didn't have any family?" she asked softly.

"Not really." He shifted and took in a breath. "I had a few good foster homes. A couple of foster parents who cared about what happened to me. One of my foster dads gave me my first job." He found a smile. "Got me into sales, actually."

She returned his smile with a small one of her own. "And that led you to working for Bill Chapman?"

"Sure did."

"But you're not in touch with any of them? Your foster families, that is?"

"Christmas cards. Some, anyway. Since I've been working at Chapman, and had a steady address for the last three years, a few of the cards actually found me. I tried to send one in return when I could."

"You'll be in Cypress Corners for Christmas," she said.

The memories of the lonely Christmases he'd spent in Boston, once he was on his own and working for a real living, were nothing to talk about. A few greeting cards were the extent of decorations in his apartment, even over the last few years.

"With all of the Fall Festival decorations I've seen going up in the town square over the past few days? I'm a little scared about just what a Cypress Corners Christmas looks like."

She laughed, tossing her head back. "Believe me, they go all out. We might not get a white Christmas down here but I bet you won't miss the snow."

"I won't miss Boston snow. Not in the city. Gray and slushy and then brown and icy. Not exactly the picture postcard New England holiday."

He stopped himself before sharing the lovely tidbit that the one Christmas with his mother he remembered, or thought he remembered, was cold and dirty and not even a little bit merry.

"So you'll be sending out Christmas cards with palm trees on them this year?" she teased.

"I guess." He arched a brow. "Maybe I should file a change of address with the Post Office."

"So those cards from your foster parents can find you?"

He shrugged in answer.

She tilted her head to one said. "There are worse things than keeping in touch with family, Eli. I might bitch and moan about it, but I love knowing I have them in my life."

"Family? They're not family."

She blinked. "They're not?"

"Nope. I have no fucking clue how to do family." He

snorted. "It's a good thing I've never really had to learn."

Caro leaned toward him, her gaze searching his face. He tried to put on his usual mask, and figured he succeeded a little when she patted his hand and sat back.

"So what are we doing on Sunday?" she asked.

"Then we're seeing each other, Cupcake?"

She smiled, her eyes sparkling. "If that's what you want to call it, that's okay with me."

"Just each other?" he asked her.

"Sounds good."

It sounded damn good to him, as surprising as that should be. At this second she looked soft and sweet, and he was damned if he didn't want to drag her out to his truck and see just how much they could manage to do without a bed. He did still have that blanket, though.

"I'd ask you to come home with me but you're working tomorrow," he said.

He saw the flash of regret in her eyes before she nodded. "At the butt-crack of dawn."

"I'll be setting up my place. Maybe you can come over tomorrow night?"

A slow smile lifted one corner of her lush mouth. "You'll

have all of your furniture, Eli."

"Yep. All of it."

"Even your Sleep Star Beauty?"

He chuckled at the ridiculous name of his new mattress.

"Yep. Do you think I could get that hug then, Cupcake?"

"I anticipate some hugging, Graham Cracker."

Chapter 13

Caro stepped out of the front of the bakery on Saturday afternoon, a bag of the now-perfected pumpkin walnut spice biscotti in her hand. She left Jane to lock up and set the alarm, and figured she would stop into the coffee shop to get herself and Eli each a drink, since she didn't know if he'd had the chance to point-and-click himself a new coffee maker yet. These particular biscotti were expressly for Eli, and she knew he'd love them. She wanted to put a smile on that handsome face of his ever since seeing the tiniest glimpse of the sad boy he'd been.

They'd texted a few times throughout the day, and he'd even stopped by to say hello. To break up his day of cleaning and heavy lifting, he'd said. The heavy-lifting she could easily believe. He'd worn a pair of those loose basketball shorts again with another sleeveless T. His hair was mussed and his face ruddy, and she'd barely refrained from jumping over the counter and kissing him silly.

Jane had questioned her in the kitchens, and Ashlyn had done likewise in the dining area. They'd both stage-whispered, which was fruitless. This was Cypress, after all. Caro was sure that half the town knew she was seeing Eli by now.

"Yoo-hoo, Caroline!"

The sing-song voice of Lettie Fairfax confirmed Caro's suspicions on that count. There were quite a few people on the sidewalk despite the heat of the afternoon, and she smiled in greeting to them as she passed. She turned and strolled over to where Lettie sat beneath the crepe myrtle. She wore her usual gardening smock and a knowing smile.

"Good afternoon, Lettie."

"Hello, dear. You've been busy at work, I see."

Caro smiled as she brushed at some stray flour that dusted her T-shirt. "Yes. It's been very busy."

"And you deserve every bit of your success."

Caro dipped her head. "Thank you."

"You know, I've been watching your place since you opened your doors." Lettie winked. "I do have an excellent vantage point."

"And you do send Tom in to pick up a treat for you now and then," Caro added. "I appreciate your business."

"Oh, it's well-deserved. Those marshmallow brownies of yours are to die for. I have to limit my indulgences, however."

"Oh?" Caro thought to give Lettie a little bit of her own medicine. "Are you dating again?"

Lettie let loose with a tinkling laugh. "Heavens, no! Mr.

Fairfax had some very big shoes to fill, dear girl. If you catch my meaning."

Caro wasn't going to touch that one. "Sure."

Lettie placed her hands on her narrow waist. "I just like to keep my figure for my own sake. A woman has a reputation to uphold, you know."

"Well, I think you look wonderful."

"And you're just as good for my ego as you are for my sweet tooth."

Caro shrugged. "That's why Sweet Escape is doing so well, I think. I'm satisfying Cypress Corners' sweet tooth."

"That's not all you're satisfying," Lettie said.

Caro stilled. *And here it comes.* "I'm not sure I get what you mean."

Lettie laughed again, drawing attention from a few of the other coffee shop patrons seated in the courtyard. "Oh, Caroline. I'm talking about that gorgeous Eli Graham, is all." She held up a hand. "Not that I'm prying. Heaven knows you don't need another woman getting mixed up in your private life."

"No, I really don't," Caro said without anger.

"Mmm hmm. How is your mother these days?"

It was Caro's turn to laugh. "There isn't much you miss, is

there?"

"Not if I can help it." Lettie took a sip of her sweet tea and then set the tall cup back down. "Not if I can help it."

"I will say this, Lettie. Eli and I are dating. But that's all I'll say."

Lettie gave a sharp nod. "Good for you. A woman deserves to keep her secrets, even one as fine as that big blond hunk of man."

"Speaking of, I'm bringing him some of the treats we're planning to sell at the Fall Festival."

"You're not holding out on me, are you?"

Caro clicked her tongue as she shrugged. "I'm afraid I am. But I will tell you one thing. You will just love these."

"I bet I will." Lettie waved a hand at her. "Now go on and get to that young man of yours. I imagine he has an appetite to go along with all of those muscles."

She shouldn't indulge Lettie. She knew this. But she couldn't resist giving her just a little bit of fuel for her fire.

"He sure does."

Lettie's laughter followed her all the way into the coffee shop.

When she stood on Eli's front porch a little while later, the pressed cardboard cup holder tray and bag of biscotti balanced with one hand, she glanced down. She should have stopped home to change, but that might have caught her mother's attention. Oh, well. Lettie had said she's entitled to her secrets, not that this one would keep for very much longer.

Eli opened the door with a wide smile. "Hey, there."

He'd changed since she'd seen him last, and now wore cargo shorts and a vintage-looking T. He'd showered too. His hair was still damp, the blond waves appearing a little bit darker. He hadn't shaved, but that wasn't a mistake in her considered opinion. She really liked his golden stubble.

"Hey, yourself." She held up the tray. "I brought sustenance."

He bent over to sniff at the bag before planting a kiss on her. Then he grinned. "Smells good, but not as good as you."

She licked her lips, savoring his taste for a second before stepping inside. "Did you get all of your work done?"

"Yep." He closed the door behind her and took the tray. "Take a look around."

The slightly dusty smell she'd caught the last time she was here was gone, and the kitchen sparkled. The wood floors glowed warmly, too. He was clearly a guy used to taking care of himself.

Glancing toward the great room, she saw it now boasted a brown leather couch and a couple of chairs in a lighter shade of tan. The coffee table was one of those industrial-looking things with thick metal legs and handles. A huge flat-screen TV hung over the fireplace and there was a squat glass lamp on an end table made to resemble a crate.

There was a table and four chairs set in the dining area of the great room, done in dark wood and surrounded by some galvanized metal chairs that she noticed matched the three tall stools now hugging the raised counter. There was little in the way of decorations, but she figured he'd grab some of those online too. There were pillows on the couch, and they were huge and looked like brushed corduroy.

"Boy, did you shop at the testosterone store?" she teased.

He chuckled as he took the lids off of their coffees. "Hey, I know what I like." He handed her the latte and sipped at his coffee. "And you apparently do, too."

"I got you an Americano. I remembered you ordered a plain coffee that first day in the bakery. Besides, you don't strike me as a caramel macchiato kind of guy."

"Not even a little bit." He went back to the counter and

hefted the bag in one hand. "Is this what I think it is?"

She nodded. "Yep. You get the first official taste."

His eyes twinkled and she just shook her head. She watched as he withdrew one of the white-chocolate-drizzled cookies and took a bite. "Oh my God," he mumbled around a mouthful of nuts and cookie.

"You like them?"

He swallowed and nodded. "These are killer, Cupcake."

"Thanks." She sipped her latte and sighed. "I think they'll do well."

"You know you'll have to top them somehow."

"What? Why?"

"For the Holiday Festival, or whatever it's called. I assume Cypress has one."

"Two, actually." His eyes widened and she laughed. "Okay, one is just for the kids but yeah, there are technically two festivals."

He finished his cookie and grabbed another. "Do you want one?"

She raised a hand. "Please. I've eaten enough of those to last me until Thanksgiving."

He brought his biscotti and coffee to the couch and sat,

leaning back with an expression of bliss on his face. She'd seen that look before. After she'd given him a little bit of pleasure the other night.

She settled beside him and drank her coffee. "We already have a biscotti for the Holiday Festival, actually. Peppermint biscotti with almonds, drizzled in dark chocolate."

He gaped at her. "Damn, I bet they're good."

"Just keep up your workouts, Graham Cracker. I plan to spoil you with sweets."

***

He grinned and set his cup on the table before wiping the crumbs from his hands. "You're the sweetest, baby."

She put her cup down and kissed him then, pressing her palms against his face. He wrapped an arm around her waist and turned, deftly pinning her beneath him. His new couch was very nice and comfy, and all the soft curves of her body pressed lusciously into his. He kissed her, and then nuzzled the crook of her neck.

"Mmm, sweet," he rasped.

"Eli." She breathed him in, running her hands over his back. "You smell so good."

"You feel good, Caro."

187

He reached up and gently tug the ponytail holder out of her hair. Then he was kissing her again, running his fingers through her hair and pulling just slightly. It felt amazing, having his hands on her in this almost-innocent way. She reached down for the hem of his T-shirt and slid her hands beneath the fabric, up over his belly to his pecs. Her fingers danced over his skin, her nails lightly raking him.

He growled and held himself up. "This is dumb. I have a brand new bed upstairs."

She giggled, but the sound was low and a little husky. "It's four thirty in the afternoon."

He snorted. "I didn't take you for a prude, Cupcake."

"I'm not a prude, wise guy." She flicked one of his nipples with her thumb nail and he sucked in a breath. "We have to save something for next time."

He swallowed another groan and kissed her again. He toed off his sneakers and reached down to slip off hers, too. It wouldn't take much to get her naked on his new couch. She seemed to be in agreement, since she pushed his shirt off like she had last time and tugged at the waistband of his shorts.

He was rock hard already, and had been halfway there since she'd walked into his new house. Her sweet scent, and the

188

bakery smells she'd brought in with her, combined to make every part of him crave a taste.

Her khakis were on the floor and he ran a hand over her sleek, strong legs. They were long for a woman of her height, and smoothly-muscled. Her little lace panties were damp as he stroked her, and she let out that soft sigh that threatened to turn him inside out.

He moved to her breasts, now covered in nothing but a matching lacy bra. Running his tongue over her flesh, he made her squirm.

"Y-yes," she said, her nails biting into his shoulders.

Giving her what he knew she craved, he suckled one pert nipple through the lace. He was going to make her come, and fast. He had to give her something before taking anything for himself. Pushing the cups of her bra aside, he palmed her perfect tits. After taking a good long look, he glanced up at her face. Her lips were parted and her eyes a dark blue now. He gently pinched her nipples and she moaned.

Covering a bare nipple with his lips, he tugged and sucked as he slid first one then two fingers inside her. She was slick and hot, and as she parted her legs to him his mouth followed his fingers to taste her again. It only took a few well-placed licks to send her over the edge. Holding on to her trembling body, he kept up the pleasure until she purred.

"Oh, Eli." Her voice was husky again, and stroked him like her fingers did. "You make me feel so good."

He sat up, bringing her with him. "I can't tell you how good you look, Cupcake. Feeling so good."

Her cheeks were pink and her eyes bright. He caught a glimmer in those eyes and she reached out to grab his dick. "I'm not leaving you wanting, Eli." A long, sure stroke made him shudder. "Not this time."

She pushed at his shoulders and he found himself with the view of her beautiful face between his thighs. Settling on her knees, she unzipped his shorts and held him like she had the other night. When she licked her lips, though? He knew he was in for more than another fantastic hand job. Lowering her head, she went to work and he couldn't restrain his moans if he tried.

"Caro," he growled, tunneling his fingers into her silky hair. "Your mouth. God."

She made the sweetest sounds as she drove him crazy, her hands and lips bringing him so close to the edge. He tried to hold on. Fisted his hands as he tried to delay his orgasm. In the end, he opened his eyes again and watched as he gave up the struggle and came hard. She took him all, finally sitting back with a pert expression on her face.

"You liked that, Eli," she said softly.

He swallowed as his breathing began to slow. "I loved that, Caro."

She was grinning as she dressed, and he could barely rouse the energy to tuck his cock back where it belonged. When she cuddled against his side, using the remote to switch through the channels on his new TV, he had the impression that he could get used to this. To having her here. She'd said they were saving his new bed for next time? He'd make sure next time was all it could be.

After that, who knew? He didn't want to think any further ahead than next week. To anticipate anything more?

That would just bite him in the ass.

Chapter 14

Sunday morning came, and with it Caro's mother bearing bagels. Caro popped a coffee pod into the machine and tried to focus on what her mother was saying. It was tough, and without a dose of caffeine she was seriously dragging.

"...attending the Fall Festival alone next weekend."

"Hmm?" Caro rubbed a hand over her face. "What?"

"I heard through the grapevine that you're dating?"

Caro bit her lower lip to keep a tell-tale smile from escaping. She was dating, all right. She'd spent a few hours dating Eli's brains out last night. They hadn't been in his new bed. She had to hold something back, didn't she? But his new couch allowed for a lot of serious messing around before she'd finally dozed tucked cozily in his strong arms.

"Yes." Caro turned and busied herself with the coffee, popping in another pod for her mother. "I'm dating."

Her mother made a sound Caro hadn't heard her make before. It was a cross between a gasp and a squeak and, bracing herself, Caro faced her again. Her mother was smiling so wide and her eyes were so bright she resembles a cartoon character.

"Oh, I'm so happy!" she cried.

Caro held up a hand as she took a sip of her coffee. Taking

in a breath, she held the mug in both hands now. "We're just dating, Mom. Don't go getting all excited."

"But you haven't dated, Caroline. Not in three years."

Caro nodded. "I know. Not really, anyway."

Her mother hopped up on one of the two barstools at the counter, folding her hands in front of her like an eager schoolgirl. "So what is it about this guy?"

Caro served her mother's coffee, pouring in the dollop of creamer she liked, and leaned on her side of the counter to face her. "Your grapevine didn't fill you in, Mom?"

Her mother blushed, actually blushed, and Caro had her answer. Lettie had given her mother an earful, apparently.

"Did Lettie call you?"

Her eyes strayed to the wall behind Caro. "She might have."

Caro couldn't get mad. Not this morning, anyway. Eli had given her three orgasms last night, so she figured that was the reason she was in such a good mood. Heck, she felt way better than she did after yoga. Not that she hadn't put some of those poses to use with Eli. Mmm.

"He's handsome, she says," her mother went on. "Big and strong?"

Caro blinked rapidly to clear her mind of the image of just how big and just how strong he was. "Yes."

"What of his family, Caro? He's from Boston?"

She could only answer one of her mother's questions. Eli's upbringing was his secret to tell, and she felt privileged that he'd told her a little bit about growing up in the foster care system.

"He's from Boston, yes." She spread some cream cheese on one half of an everything bagel. "He worked for Bill Chapman, remember."

"Ooh, he's a tough one. Your father says that he's got brass balls."

Caro nearly spit her coffee out on that one. "W-what?"

"He's a tough business man, Caro. Loosen up, will you?"

"Me?" She gaped at her mother. "You want me to loosen up?"

"Or something. You're always wound so tight." Her head tilted slightly and her eyes narrowed. "Although you look different this morning. I don't know what it is."

"I'm still tired, Mom." Her cheeks burned but she kept her expression even. "It was a busy week, thank God, and this is the one day I get to sleep in."

"And that's why I don't drop by until after nine on

194

Sundays."

Caro had to give her that one. Nine o'clock sounded very late to her, since she normally rose at four every other morning.

"Your sister is coming to the festival," her mother went on. "She's bringing the girls, of course."

"Oh, they'll love it!"

Sherry had two little girls, Libby who was eleven years old and Justine who was eight. Or Liberty and Justice, as they were called. They were the sweetest things, blond and bright and very curious like their mother.

"I'm going to try to talk her into letting the girls stay over on the weekend."

"I'm sure Sherry won't mind, Mom."

"You know your sister, Caroline."

That wasn't exactly true, since Sherry was twelve years older and had been pretty much doing her own thing while Caro was growing up.

"Maybe she'll want a little alone time with Paul?"

Her mother straightened. "Yes! You know, your father and I have that gift certificate to a resort hotel up in Orlando. It's from a very grateful client. Anyway, maybe Sherry and Paul would like to use it."

Caro gave a noncommittal shrug. "Sure. Sounds like a plan."

"Yes, that's what I'll do." She beamed at Caro. "Caroline, sometimes you have the best ideas! Like opening your bakery. Or dating that gorgeous guy."

Caro winked. "So he's gorgeous now? How do you know?"

"Lettie, dear. She told me he practically gave her the vapors with his charming manners, even though he *is* a Yankee. Her words."

Caro laughed as she took another bite of her bagel. "That sure sounds like Lettie."

"Does he give you the vapors?"

Her mother's question sounded light but she knew what the woman was asking. Caro hadn't really dated anyone since the accident, and having her heart broken was only one reason. Guilt and grief weren't very good for the soul, but she was only just starting to dig herself out from under them.

"Eli makes me laugh, Mom. He's not a serious-relationship kind of guy and that's just what I'm looking for right now."

"You're just hooking up?"

"Mom!"

"Well, isn't that what it's called? I watch those bachelor shows, you know."

"We're not just hooking up." She thought for a second. "I'm not sure what we're doing, but while we're doing it we're not seeing other people."

Her mother gave a nod. "Good. That's something. When can I meet him?"

"Oh, no. No family dinners, Mom. If you want to meet him, go to the Sales Center. He's there Monday through Friday."

"Maybe I will."

"Don't you dare!"

"Caroline! You'd think I was going to do something to embarrass you."

"Aren't you?"

"Probably. You do embarrass fairly easily." She stepped off the barstool, brushing her hands over her jeans. "I'll leave you to your Sunday then, dear."

She bent to kiss Caro's cheek and then left. Caro looked at the spread in front of her and got a delicious idea. Bagging up the bagels and capping the spreads, she smiled to herself. He'd said he was a morning person, didn't he?

Taking a quick shower and dressing in denim capris and a

soft yellow top, she slipped on her Keds and made her way down to her car. Maybe she shouldn't just drop by, but she only had her Sundays free. And she wanted to spend them with the one person who did, indeed, give her the vapors.

***

Eli's feet pounded to a stop as he checked his fitness tracker. A ten K today. Not bad. He'd passed the Adventure Trails Jake Chapman had created, and made a mental note to give them a try soon. Caro kept pretty fit. Maybe they could climb a wall or something together.

Slowing as he cooled down, he thought about last night with her. They'd done just about everything you could do without actually closing the deal, but he wasn't frustrated in the least. She was sensual and giving, and sweetly funny too. It was weird, having this semi-relationship thing with a woman. He liked having her in his space, though. That alone was a first for him.

As he neared the townhouses he spied her little green mini parked in front of his house. With a grin splitting his face, he picked up his pace and saw that she sat on his stoop. It wasn't a porch. Not really. It needed a doormat and a bench or something. It was still just a square of concrete with a roof jutting out above it.

"Hey, Cupcake."

She stood, holding a white paper bag in her arms. "I brought you some breakfast. I didn't know you'd be out running."

"Have you been waiting long?"

She shook her head, her blond curls looking wild and soft this morning. "I should have called."

"I wouldn't have answered." He stretched a little, preening as he flexed his legs. "I was in the zone."

Smiling, she patted the bag. "I brought you carbs. Bagels from the market, courtesy of my mother."

"Your mother?"

"She likes to bring them by my apartment every Sunday morning."

"And to check for any wayward guys who might have gotten lost there on Saturday night, I'm guessing?"

"I've never had a guy in my apartment."

That surprised him. Not that he thought she was an easy mark. Just that she lived alone and was smoking hot.

"Their loss." He stepped closer and bent to kiss her. "I stink."

"Not yet, but you will."

"Then come inside while I shower and then I'll let you carb me up."

He let her inside and left her downstairs while he took the fastest shower in his memory. As tempted as he was to take her upstairs with him, he sensed she wasn't ready for that yet. They'd yet to sleep together, after all. His cock hardened a little as he recalled all the other things they'd done to and for each other. And what they'd do tonight if things went his way.

Toweling off a little roughly to bring himself into control, he quickly dressed in jeans and a T-shirt. When he joined her downstairs he found her perched on one of the barstools, her feet tapping as she rested her chin in one hand. She'd obviously found the new dishes he'd washed and put in the cabinets and the tall counter was set. It was homey and like nothing he was used to. She looked really good in his space though, and the thought struck him as strange. Jeez, somebody would think he was getting used to living here in Cypress and it had only been a couple of weeks.

"Bagel me, Cupcake."

"That might be the strangest sentence I've ever heard." She smiled as she held up the dish piled with bagels of a couple different varieties. "Pick what you like. I ate an everything, myself."

"Sounds good. Is there another one?"

"Mmm hmm. I don't know what my mother is thinking, but she always brings me too many bagels for just myself."

"Maybe she's not checking on you, Caro. Maybe she's hoping to find somebody there with you on a Sunday morning."

She shrugged, her lips quirked in a half-smile. "Maybe."

He took a bagel and chewed. "Mmm. Good. You don't make these?"

"Nope. There's something about the dough that just isn't in my wheelhouse."

"It's good to know your strengths."

She looked like she wanted to ask him more about that but he quickly closed it down with a wink.

"Remind me to show you mine later," he added.

"Don't get ahead of yourself, Graham Cracker." She sipped at her coffee. "So what's our Sunday look like?"

"I have an idea, but I don't know if you'll be up for it."

She turned her stool and crossed her arms. "Is this another dare?"

He nodded as he thought about the attraction he'd heard

about from some visitors to Cypress on Friday. "Since you liked the Ferris wheel at Old Town Village, maybe you'll be up to riding the really big one they built up in Orlando?"

Her eyes went round and she covered her mouth. "That's really tall, Eli."

"Are you afraid, Cupcake?"

She swallowed. "If you can take it, so can I."

"Now there's the attitude I like." He leaned down and kissed her, pulling back to grin. "It'll be handy to have for later."

She laughed but he saw her eyes darken. Just what was she thinking? He ate his bagel and drained his coffee, eager to start their day together. So that they could finish it right here.

Later that night, they were curled up on his couch again. He could almost hear the clock ticking down on their day, since she had to get up so early in the morning tomorrow. They'd had a lot of fun up in Orlando, and now shared a pizza ordered from the tavern.

"You know, my house is so much closer to the bakery than yours is," he said.

She shook her head. "Not going to happen. Besides, you don't want somebody invading your space. You just moved in."

"I like having you in my space, Cupcake."

She blushed prettily and gently stroked his leg. "That's actually very sweet."

He ran his fingers through her hair and massaged the back of her neck. "You're actually very sweet."

She gave his thigh a squeeze and patted him. "I should get going, though."

"Yeah, the reality of dating a baker."

"Whoa, you said the D word."

"Aren't we dating?" He wasn't playing dumb or cute. He'd just never really dated a woman like her.

Her brows drew together before she nodded. "We are. I told my mother we're seeing each other, but I'll take the upgrade."

Her agreement made him lighter inside somehow. He had to be careful. For her sake and for his. He wasn't a forever guy, seeing as he'd never had to be. She was a forever girl, though. Even if she might say otherwise.

He wouldn't think about it now. Not when she was rubbing her hand along his thigh and looking at him with that heat in her blue-green eyes. He could set it aside for now, if his now included her. As for his later?

He'd roll with the disappointment like he always did.

Chapter 15

"All set for the Fall Festival?"

Caro looked up from the customer in front of her to find Claire Chapman standing over near the bake cases.

"If you're asking about my biscotti, then yes."

She clasped her hands. "Yay! Make sure and set aside a large order for me, Caro. I plan on eating this baby's weight in them."

Caro eyed her round belly and smiled. "You got it."

The festival was the next day, on Saturday, and Cypress clearly expected a big crowd. The town square was decorated with hay bales and pumpkins and piles and piles of colorful silk maple leaves scattered among the dried brown leaves that fell from the sycamore trees in Cypress. Sweet Escape wouldn't be left out, of course. Ashlyn and Caro had turned it out while Jane baked batch after batch of their customers' favorites as well as the new cookies. Blockades stood folded and ready to close off the roads around the square to everything but foot traffic and volunteers were beginning to tape off the areas where vendors would set up.

The bakery had been very busy all day, too. Caro hummed to herself as she assisted another customer. She felt pretty good, even if she'd had to face the fact that she was dating Eli. Their Sunday together had been eye-opening, and not just because they'd ridden one of the tallest Ferris wheels in the world. The one up in Orlando was identical to one built in London, and she figured their view from the top was just as impressive. Hey, London didn't have the house of mouse, now did they? And what was Big Ben compared to a fantasy castle?

Still, it was clear that Eli had no clue how to do the dating thing. Or at least, he believed he didn't. He was courteous and affectionate all day, and at night? After sharing their dinner of pizza they'd fooled around again. Although he'd teased her enough about his new big bed, they hadn't quite made it up there. He was clearly waiting for a signal from her, not that she even knew what that could be. She alternated between ready and willing to abject cowardice.

It would be amazing, being with Eli. How could it not be? He knew just about every inch of her body now, and let her explore him too. There was something so unnerving about the thought of actually having sex with a guy, even a guy as sweet and hot as Eli. She hadn't been with anyone since Brad, and after losing her baby she'd begun to think that nothing and no one could make her feel that kind of desire again. And then in walked Eli. Swaggered, more like. He had confidence in spades and was clearly willing to wait for her to give him permission or something. To wait until she was ready.

"I'm so ready," she murmured.

"What's that, dear?"

She looked up to find Sharon Walsh in front of her. Ty's mother, one of her mother's friends, smiled sweetly at her.

"Hello, Mrs. Walsh. What can I get you?"

"A couple of cupcakes for my granddaughter. Ty is picking her up this afternoon and we get her for the whole weekend!"

Riley was the daughter of Mrs. Walsh's late daughter, but Ty and his wife Cassie had her more weekends than not. Sharon always seemed to bloom when her little granddaughter was around.

"She'll have so much fun at the festival," Caro said as she filled her order.

"Yes. You seem a little distracted, Caro. But you're ready. Rest assured."

Caro's mouth dropped open. "How can you know that?"

Sharon patted her hand. "It's a very big deal, but you'll do fine. You'll see."

Caro's cheeks burned as she stared at Ty's mother.

"What?"

"The festival, dear. You made it through last year's, didn't
you?"

"Yes." She let out a little laugh. "Yes. We are ready. I'm
just going over the preparations in my head."

Sharon paid for the cupcakes and took her box of goodies.
"Don't you fret, dear. It'll all turn out fine in the end."

Caro just nodded, finding so much more meaning in the
woman's words than she'd probably intended. She should go for
it with Eli. He was a good guy deep down. She had that slime
ball radar after all, and he never even caused a blip. He was a
temporary sort of guy, though. She couldn't ignore that.
Everything he had was rented! Stamped with an expiration date.
She didn't want to look too far into the future herself. Did she?

"Almost closing time, boss," Jane said as she stepped out
of the kitchen. "Then you and I can get going on those finishing
touches."

"Yep."

She didn't expect that she would get to see Eli tonight. Her
business was her priority and tomorrow was a big day for Sweet
Escape. Hers was the newest business in the town center and,
even though she wasn't a lawyer or law professor like her

siblings, she wanted her business to be the best. To excel. She wanted to be a success and to make her family proud.

She wanted to have fun too, darn it. And getting closer to Eli, for however long that would be, was a great way to do it.

By the time the bakery was closed, she and Jane were up to their elbows in dough and batter and frosting. The bake case would look full to bursting with all the colors of fall tomorrow, and the flavors too. They would have a spiced apple cupcake with cinnamon frosting, savory butternut squash scones, and hearty zucchini pumpkin bread. There were more fall-themed flavors and textures in the hopefully-famous biscotti and also in a pumpkin cake with a cream cheese glaze.

They did as much of the prep work as possible ahead of time and were just cleaning up the kitchen around six o'clock when someone knocked on the door. She peeked out toward the front door and saw that Eli stood there. Her heart did a silly little flip thing she'd noticed just a few days ago. She tamped down her excitement. He was just stopping by. That's all.

She crossed to the door and opened it. "Hey, we're closed mister."

"I know." He bent down and kissed her, making her pulse kick. "I knew you'd be busy and would forget about dinner."

He held a bag of takeout from the tavern and she could smell beef and cheese and French fries. "Oh, you're a doll man!"

"A what?"

She laughed. "Sorry. That just slipped out."

"I brought a burger for Jane, too."

"Thanks, Eli," Jane said, peeking out of the kitchen. "My hubby is making dinner for me."

"Then you'll have to eat with me," Caro told him.

He raised his eyebrows. "Are you sure? Don't you two have a lot of baker-elf things to get finished for tomorrow?"

"We've done all we can tonight," Caro said.

"And on that note, I'm heading home." Jane waved and ducked out the back door.

***

While Caro went into the kitchen to lock the door behind Jane, Eli set up their impromptu dinner. He'd been busy all day, and he was surprised to see that a couple of his tours were recent prospective residents who'd asked for him specifically. One was a couple in their fifties looking to move into the green neighborhood and the other that family that had given him such rave reviews last week. They were eager to get their two children into the neighborhood school, so they wanted him to find a rental property where they could live while narrowing down which of the villages in Cypress would best suit them.

Another unique aspect of Cypress Corners was that the Sales Center dealt with residents and properties, both resale and new. They also handed rentals. This helped property owners by giving them a hand both in finding tenants and in case anything unfortunate occurred, like skipping out on their lease, property damage or excess neighbor complaints. Currently they referred any legal issues that might arise, but Bill Chapman had mentioned the possibility of putting one of his legal eagles in place. Eli was really grateful that he wasn't one of them. Derek could have that distinction, thanks.

"This is a nice surprise."

Caro walked in, sending thoughts of Bill or Derek right out of his mind. She looked rumpled and a little tired, but she wore it well.

"I was thinking about you all day," he admitted.

Her brows rose, and then a gorgeous smile curved her lips. "You have that going on too, then?"

Her question made his chest tighten, but it wasn't an uncomfortable sensation. It was one that was starting to feel familiar where she was concerned. He just had to think about her and he was filled with this warm sensation. Yeah, she got his dick hard but it was more than that. He wanted to make her smile, and it seemed like she was enjoying spending time together too.

"Come eat, Cupcake."

She sat down at the little round table and let out a sigh. "Mmm, this looks so good. Thanks, Eli."

"No problem." He grabbed a few fries and chewed as she dug into her burger. "So are you all set for tomorrow?"

She nodded, her eyes bright. "Yes, all set. I have Tom from the coffee shop and Ashlyn helping us out front and Jane and I will hold down the fort in here. What about you?"

"The Sales Center is closed of course, but Rick wants us to glad-hand the place."

"Will you be giving tours?"

"Nope. We'll be taking appointments and pointing them to the website, though. Should be a pretty easy gig."

She sat back and crossed her arms, her eyes sparkling.

"What?" he had to know.

"You like this. Working in Cypress."

"I do." He shrugged. "It's no big deal. I just do what I have to do."

Something flickered in her eyes before she looked away. "Okay. Will I see you tomorrow?"

"Yeah, you will. I plan on talking your place up to everyone I meet."

Her eyes widened. "Seriously? Eli, that would be fantastic!"

"You work your ass off, Caro. You should enjoy the success you've achieved, and if I can help you gain more by simply telling the truth? Why wouldn't I?"

She jumped out of her chair and hugged him. He caught her easily, settling her on his lap as she buried her face in the crook of his neck. "You get it, don't you?" she asked softly.

"Hey." He held her slightly away from him and touched her cheek. "I know what it's like to try your best, yeah."

She bit her lip, her eyes shiny, and he couldn't resist kissing her. She was a delicious bundle in his arms, and that odd tickling in his chest moved down to his belly as she kissed him back. Heat rose between them, and he drove his tongue into her mouth. She turned to straddle him, and he welcomed the rush to his groin. She knew damn well what she did to him, and he wasn't the guy to pretend she didn't affect him. His hands were on her round little ass as she ran her fingers through his hair.

When she pulled back, her cheeks flushed, she was grinning. "You're good for me, Eli." She cupped his face, her fingers gently stroking him. "You know that, right?"

He didn't know just what she was asking him, but he could certainly answer the question on the smooth shiny surface.

"Yeah, I do." He covered one of her hands with his. "I think you're pretty good for me, too."

She let out a breath, and then yawned. "Sorry."

"Hey, you should get some sleep. Are you coming here at oh dark thirty tomorrow morning?"

"Four thirty, and yes."

He gave her ass a pat. "Then you should get home."

She looked reluctant to squeeze out of his arms, and that made him feel a whole lot more than pretty good.

By the time she was driving herself home and he was walking back to his townhouse, he'd had some time to think about what he and Caro were doing. They were dating, or so everyone in Cypress had labeled it. Jessie and Bree and even Oliver seemed to think of them as a couple. The teasing didn't bother him. It wasn't like he was scoping out the other admittedly-hot women in the office. Being linked to a woman like Caro could only be good for his cred. He was worried about what she thought about it all.

She'd said he was good for her. He didn't know about that. He'd never been good for anybody. Not good enough, anyway. Not his mother, who apparently couldn't stay clean long enough to raise her son. Not his father, who never even bothered to learn if he was one. None of his foster parents gave more than the required support and supervision, in his opinion.

"Doesn't matter," he grumbled as he let himself into his new home. "She's really good for me."

He did think about her, though. A lot. He hadn't been just giving her a line. It might be only a couple of weeks since they'd started whatever this was between them, but he was past throwing lines at her to see what stuck. What hit her just right. He'd loved her everyway but one, and he hoped that changed soon. It wasn't exactly like he was getting blue balls, was it? The girl was inventive, all right.

He yawned now himself, grabbed a bottle of beer from the fridge, and then plopped down on the big leather couch. Thumbing through channels on the TV, he tried to focus on one thing or another but just couldn't land. He wanted Caro here with him. For more than just a couple of hours of fun, too. He wanted her to stay the night, for God's sake. That thought alone should make his balls crawl back up inside his body.

He never let a woman stay over. Hell, that was even if he brought them back to his bed in the first place. He preferred to play every game on the road, so to speak. Not this time. Not with her.

She did live above her parents' garage, though. That put a very tricky spin on doing a road trip. He didn't want to hit and quit her, either. Which made wanting her to stay in his place seem so very strange.

"Strange or not, she's staying here tomorrow night," he murmured.

Let somebody else worry about what this step meant. He wouldn't wait for someone at the Sales Center to remark on it, either. Caro's friend, and his coworker, Jessie did live just a few doors down. She'd know if Caro stayed over. Even if she didn't, didn't women talk about that stuff? He had no clue. He'd had no real foster sisters, and the girls in the group homes didn't spend time with the boys for obvious reasons.

There was that memory he'd had a few weeks ago, of gathering leaves with an older girl or a young woman. Even that almost intangible moment wasn't enough to give him any insight into a woman's mind. He never tried to figure out what any of them wanted, aside from a good meal and a good fuck. Caro was so different, though. Real and tangible in a way he'd never expected.

He was rooted in Cypress for the foreseeable future, and he suspected that if he hurt her he'd have a whole bunch of people to answer to for it. Besides, he couldn't imagine hanging out with any other woman here. She was here, and it was her home. It might not be his, not yet, but it was the closest he'd ever come to one. He might have to figure all of this out, but he was sure of one thing.

He was going to try his damnedest to not screw this up.

Chapter 16

At seven sharp, Ashlyn opened the front door of Sweet Escape to the tuneful five notes of its signature pop song.

"Ready, boss?" she asked, her voice squeaky with excitement.

Caro's pulse raced like she'd just run all the way here instead of driving and actually being on the premises for a couple of hours now.

"Ready." She sucked in a breath, slow and deep, and exhaled. "I don't think we'll be busy this early, but—"

Her words were cut off as a wave of customers filed inside. The vendors apparently wanted more than whatever they were selling at the festival themselves, if the buzz of conversation and the beeping of the register was any indication. Jane was grinning as she served them while Caro walked through the dining area greeting everyone.

"Where do you want me?" Tom asked her, tying one of the short green aprons around his waist.

"Do anything Ashlyn tells you to do," Caro said.

Becky's little brother grinned as his freckled cheeks turned pink. "If you insist."

Ashlyn snorted. "Boy, please."

Tom laughed as he helped her take orders by hand while Jane and Caro worked the counter.

"That guy wasn't kidding," one man said around a mouthful of s'mores brownie. "This is fantastic."

"He told me about the biscotti, miss," an older woman said. "I have to try the pumpkin walnut biscotti. It sounds amazing."

Caro felt a thrill as she realized just whom they were talking about. Eli hadn't been kidding, then.

"Hey, the guy knows what's good," Jane said with a wink. "Gotta love him."

Caro froze, and then jerked herself back into motion. She didn't love Eli, did she? No. They were dating. They'd only known each other for a couple of weeks. She liked him, though. A lot, and today's evidence of his glowing endorsement was only one reason.

"Good morning," Eli said as he shouldered his way into the bakery. "How is everybody this morning?"

"You were so right, buddy," a different man said. "This place is phenomenal."

Eli looked at Caro, that crooked grin on his face, and nodded. "Yeah, it is."

The next hour went by in a snap, and by eight o'clock she'd lost track of Eli. She could see foot traffic starting to build out on the street in front, and bit her lower lip as she debated her next move. There were booths set up across the street and all through the square. The day was bright already, and between the decorations and the number of people it looked like the festival was off to a fantastic start. Even if it hadn't officially started, anyway.

"Are you going to head out there now?" Jane asked her.

"I'm not sure." Caro answered. "The festival doesn't start until nine."

Jane peered through one of the picture windows. "It doesn't look to me like that matters much right now."

Caro had to agree with her. "How's our inventory?" she called over to Ashlyn.

"We've got this, boss," Ashlyn answered from behind the bake cases. "You and Jane have everything organized back there so Tom and I can just sell, sell, sell."

Caro grinned as Becky's little brother nodded enthusiastically. "Okay, good. I'll do a sweep and report back."

Jane shook her head at her. "Go get yourself a latte, if you can manage the crowds in the coffee shop, and head over to the

219

Sales Center."

"Why would I go to the Sales Center?"

"Because that's probably where you'll find Eli."

Caro waved a hand but she couldn't keep the smile off her face. "Oh, I wasn't looking for him."

"Yeah, you weren't," Ashlyn chimed in.

Caro clicked her tongue and walked outside with the next wave of customers happily munching on their treats.

She found Eli out in front of the Sales Center, surrounded by people and talking to them like he'd known them forever. He was really good with people, but she suspected he didn't think so. They were certainly drawn to him, men and women alike. And kids, apparently. As she watched, a little boy who looked about four years old tugged on Eli's pant leg. Eli held up a hand to the guy he'd been talking to and crouched down in front of the boy. She couldn't hear what they were saying, but Eli was laughing and the boy wore a big smile.

As she neared, he lifted his head and his eyes brightened. "Hey there, Cupcake."

The other people turned to look at her, and a couple of them chuckled.

"It's the woman from the bakery," one of the women said.

"Good one, Eli."

Eli shrugged. "So how are things at Sweet Escape?"

Caro knew why he'd worded his question that way. He was branding the bakery in front of the visitors and residents.

"Great, thanks," she said. "Our new fall items are really popular."

"The pumpkin walnut biscotti, I'll bet." He faced the others again. "Have you tried the biscotti? Man, I'm telling you."

"I had one of the brownies," a woman said. "I've never tasted anything like it."

"Just wait until you try the scones," another woman said. "They're perfect if you want something a little less sweet."

Caro was flushed from the praise and from Eli's crystal-sugar gaze on her. She mouthed a thank you to him and he nodded.

He put his hand on one guy's shoulder. "Are you guys hanging around for a hayride? They start at ten."

"Yeah, the hayride!" The little boy hopped up and down and his mother smiled down at him. "Sure, we can."

Eli reached out for Caro's hand. "We'll be taking it later, won't we?" She nodded and he drew her closer. "Now I promised this lady a cup of coffee, so if you'll excuse me?"

The others all nodded, making sounds of agreement as Eli led her back across the street.

"You promised me a cup of coffee?" she teased.

"How else was I going to get out of there? Besides, I know you want a cup of coffee."

"And you know what I want now?"

That heat flared in his gaze and then he laughed. "Nah. That one is too easy."

"That was pretty smooth back there, Graham Cracker," she said as they queued up in line at the coffee shop. "You're good at that."

"At what?"

"Talking to people. Making friends."

"They're not friends. They're prospects."

"If you say so. Seemed to me like you were all getting along."

"Yeah, we were. It's no hardship talking to the folks who come out to Cypress. They're already half sold on the place before I open my mouth."

"When they see your pretty face, you mean?"

He laughed. "Hey, I can't help it if I'm beautiful."

She smacked his shoulder. "Go on, charmer. Lettie had you pegged all right."

"Lettie fell under my charms, that's true." He leaned closer to whisper in her ear. "I'm not going to let her in on my secret, though."

"You have a secret? I thought you were an open book."

"Maybe secret isn't the right word. A surprise, maybe."

"Ooh, now you've got me."

He took her hand again and laced his fingers through hers. "I'll remind you of that later."

***

Eli ate his lunch from one of the food trucks lining one side of the town square. The fish tacos were fantastic, and he made a mental note to grab a couple more and take them to Caro. Who knew when she would allow herself to take a real break. The festival was packed and the sky had a few well-placed clouds to keep the attendees from melting into puddles on the hay-strewn sidewalks.

Grabbing a cup of coffee with Caro had been fun, but he knew she was too wrapped up in the bakery to give him any more time than that. When he stopped by to take her some lunch he would look into giving her a hand. If what he'd been hearing all morning was true, she'd be sold out long before she closed her doors. He planned to be there when that happened, and then drag her outside to have a little fun.

"Hey there, Eli," Claire Chapman called.

Eli looked up to see Claire and her husband Jake walking toward him.

"Hey," he said in answer.

"We haven't officially met," Jake said, sticking out his hand. "Jake Chapman."

"Eli Graham, Jake." He shook his hand. "Nice to meet you."

Jake nodded. "Have you seen my brother? Rick, that is."

Eli shook his head. "Last I saw him he was out by the bounce house with Nick."

Nick was his boss's little boy. The kid was pretty cool, as far as little kids went. Eli found he liked it when Rick's wife Harmony brought the boy by the Sales Center for a visit. Nick looked like a mini-me of Rick, and it was always surprising to see how his usually-unflappable boss got almost silly with his son.

"I figured." Jake ran his gaze over him and Eli did likewise. The guy looked a lot like his brother. Both his brothers, actually. "So when are you going to come out to the Adventure Trails?"

"Not sure," Eli said. "I've been thinking about it, though."

Jake nodded. "I saw you out running around town, so I figured you could use the challenge."

Claire smacked Jake in the shoulder in that oddly feminine way that Caro had done to him before. "Not everyone needs to cheat death every day, Jake."

"No death-cheating required." Jake splayed a hand on his chest. "If you need something a little more tame, my sister Cassie runs the Kids' programs."

Eli chuckled. "I think I can handle anything you dish out, man."

Jake's eyes sparkled. "Hey, I like this guy."

Claire smiled. "I thought you might. He's got your…oh, what's the word?"

"Self-confidence?" Eli provided.

"Charisma?" Jake offered.

Claire snorted. "Inflated sense of self."

Eli and Jake both laughed at that.

"So how are the fish tacos?" Jake asked.

"Really good. Everything I've eaten today has been great."

"Especially the biscotti from Sweet Escape," Claire said, rubbing her round belly. "Jake bought enough to get me through the day."

"I bought enough to get you through the week," Jake said.

Claire shook her head. "The baby wants what the mama wants, and I likes my pumpkin spice."

"It's a good thing you grabbed some while you could," Eli said. "I think Caro will be sold out of just about everything pretty soon."

Claire beamed. "I'm so happy for her. She's worked so hard to get that business off the ground. She could take more time off, though."

"I agree." Eli winked. "Hopefully I can get her to just enjoy the festival when she's free."

"You know, I think you're good for her," Claire said. "She could use some fun in her life."

She brightened as she glanced across the street. "Oh, there's Tammy." She grabbed Jake's hand. "See you later, Eli!"

Claire dragged her husband over toward Tammy Chapman, where she stood with her husband Ben and a baby stroller. Eli finished his lunch and wiped his hands, his mind on what Claire had said. Caro had told him he was good for her, too. He did

226

bring some fun into her life, but he couldn't help but wonder if there might be more to it than that.

Before he could get too introspective, he found the little boy he'd seen earlier today standing at his table.

"Hi, Eli," he said.

"Hi, Josh." He had a knack for remembering names, which served him very well in his line of work. "Where are your parents?"

Josh pointed to the right and Eli saw that his mother and father stood close by at the taco truck, their eyes on their son. They both waved at him and Eli returned the gesture. He looked back at Josh. The little boy was digging into a box of chicken nuggets.

"No tacos, Josh?"

Josh wrinkled his nose. "No."

"So you're a chicken nugget man, then."

Josh grinned. "Yep."

His parents came over to join them. "Josh, are you bothering Eli?" his mother asked.

"Not at all." Eli smiled. "Have you been in the bounce house?"

Josh nodded. "Oh, yeah."

"What about the kids' course over at the Adventure Trails?"

Josh's eyes went round but his mother shook her head.

"Oh, no," she said.

"Come on," Josh's dad said. "Josh can handle it. Right, Eli?"

"I believe he can. They're completely supervised. Very safe."

"I don't know…" the mom said.

"Honey, if Eli says Josh can handle it," the dad began. "That he'll be safe? We can trust that."

Eli couldn't say anything to that. He simply nodded and returned Josh's high-five before the little boy went off with his parents to eat their lunch at a nearby table. These people he'd known for just a few days, a family he was trying to sell on Cypress, trusted what he said? Jesus, no one had ever said anything like that to him before.

Grabbing up his trash, he dumped it in the closest can and started walking toward the bakery. He was making connections here in Cypress, like Bill Chapman had wanted and Eli fully expected. He'd always been the one who didn't make waves. Who became whatever his foster parents needed him to be. A people-pleaser.

He was all charm and shine, and had a knack for figuring out just what people needed from him. He gave it, too. Now that he was a grown-ass man, he knew how desperate he'd been to find his own place. Now he used his particular skills to make his living. As for a life? Maybe he'd try to have one of those someday.

For now, he'd make his money and make connections. Family? He'd never had one. Friends? Hell, he'd never really had any of them either.

He pulled open the door to Sweet Escape and heard the now-familiar chime. He chose to focus on the one connection that was suddenly the most important right now.

"Hey there, Cupcake."

She turned to him and smiled, and his lungs seized. He wouldn't try to figure out why he felt better just breathing in her space.

It had to be the sugar.

Chapter 17

"This is Caro Richmond taking a break?" he teased her.

She stretched out on his couch and grinned, looking more relaxed than he'd seen her in several days. "This is Caro Richmond having fun."

"You're having fun with me." He gave her a quick kiss and clinked his wine glass to hers. "I had a lot of it with you today."

"I liked hanging out with you at the festival, Eli."

"Yeah? I was surprised I was able to drag you away."

"Sweet Escape officially sold out around two o'clock, in no small part thanks to you and your not-so-subtle promotion. And since Jane and I have less prep to do on Saturdays, we finished up and called it a day."

He shook his head. "My promo might have had something to do with it, but I think at least some of the thanks goes to Claire Chapman's little bundle."

Caro shrugged. "Claire likes her sweets. That's for sure. She's a great baker too, but I think I actually managed to make something she couldn't. Not yet, anyway."

"She's your biggest fan." He winked, a crooked smile on his face. "Well, maybe your second biggest."

She blushed at his backhanded confession, but he couldn't

tell if she believed him or not. "It was nice just walking around and enjoying the festival, though. I don't think I would have done that if it wasn't for you."

That surprised him. "Why not? You've got a lot of friends in Cypress."

"But they have their families now, most of them anyway. Or families on the way."

He tilted his head and blinked at her. "Your family was there too, Caro. Your sister seems nice. And I thought your nieces were too cute. Liberty and Justice. Lawyers in the making, I'll bet."

"If my dad has his way." Her gaze drifted to the contents of her wine glass. "I don't get to see them half as much as I'd like to."

There was something in her voice, a wistfulness that he'd never heard before. It held a note of sadness, too. Like the time he'd found her asleep in the swing out by the lake.

"Your sister lives up in Orlando, right?"

"Just north of it. My brother Robbie lives up that way too. They both work at the family firm in downtown Orlando."

"You have a brother?"

"Two, actually. Phillip is a law professor."

Eli let out a low whistle and gave a nod. Wow. She came from a family of highly successful people. She deserved every bit of success she'd carved out for herself. That was for sure.

"You live at your parents' place," he held up a hand to stop her when she looked like she was going to correct him. "Sorry, *above* your parents' place. They don't come for those dreaded family dinners you told me about?"

A shadow of a smile lifted her lips. "They have their lives, Eli. They've almost always had lives separate from mine." She shrugged again. "I was a surprise."

"They're older than you?"

"Way older."

He took the wine glass from her hand and set it and his on the coffee table. "You were a surprise for me too, Cupcake."

She folded her legs beneath her and turned to face him. "I was?"

"Yep. A good one, too." Wrapping an arm around her, he drew her closer. "Unexpected, and just what I needed."

Her eyes were that dark shade of blue he loved, the color he noticed they turned right before she kissed him. He flattered himself that he was able to drag her mind from her slightly-separate siblings.

232

"You're just what I need, Eli." Her arms went around his neck and she brought her body up against his. "Right now."

Right now. He could do right now. It was later he wasn't so great at.

"Are you finally going to try out my new bed with me?"

She gave a nod, bringing her face to his. "Are you up for it?"

He laughed low in his throat. "Ah, Caro. That one is way too easy."

She leaned her head back and he took the opportunity to nuzzle her throat. Her scent wrapped around him, caught in her skin and in her hair, and he breathed her in. His body reacted, and he welcomed the heated rush.

"Upstairs, Caro," he rasped, licking her skin. "Naked and upstairs in my bed."

She shivered in his arms and nodded. "That better not be a line, Graham Cracker."

"No line."

He kissed her, driving his tongue into her mouth and tasting her. She kissed him back, and it felt urgent and perfect and he had to get her under him. Or over him. Or in front of him. At this second, he didn't much care about the position.

Leaving a trail of clothes behind them, they kissed as they fumbled and stumbled up the stairs to his bedroom. Then he had her naked beneath him, leaning back on her elbows as she watched him strip off his pants faster than he ever had.

The room wasn't quite dark, but he didn't need much light. He'd all but memorized her body over the past couple of weeks, and tonight he would touch every inch of her. He swallowed a groan. With every inch of himself.

"Christ, Caro." He covered her on the bed, resting on his elbows as he closed his eyes. "You feel so good."

She arched beneath him, rubbing her nipples against his chest with a soft moan. "Eli."

He shifted and covered one breast with a hand while he licked and sucked her nipple. "There's so much more room up here, Cupcake."

She opened her legs wide as his hand moved over her flat belly to her curls. "Yeah, there is."

He was pounding now, his cock so ready to be inside of her. It would be their first time, though. He'd had plenty of first times, and last times, with women but this time was different. She was different. Hell, maybe even he was different.

"I've dreamed about this," he said, kissing her lips, her

234

cheek, her throat.

"I hope I don't disappoint you," she whispered, her voice so soft he could hardly hear it.

He stilled, and brought his face to hers. "Caro, trust me. There's no way in hell you could ever disappoint me."

She smiled, stretching her arms over her head. "Then take me already."

He let out a strangled laugh and kissed her again. "Be right back."

***

Caro wriggled into the very nice mattress beneath her as she waited for Eli to come back from the bathroom. She hadn't been kidding about disappointing him. It had been so long since she'd slept with a guy. The last man she'd been with was Brad, and just a few days before he died.

God, so much was tangled up in regrets about Brad. Regret that he'd been killed in that car crash. Regret that he'd been cheating on her while she'd been with him. Regret that the other woman had died too. She must not have been enough for Brad. That was obvious to her. She couldn't hold onto him, or onto their baby that was with her for such a short time.

She rubbed a hand over her face, sending Brad and their

past together out of her head. Eli was what mattered in this moment. Eli and his charming, sexy ways. He'd assured her she wouldn't disappoint him, but he was a guy right? Didn't they always feel good after?

"Sorry about that." Eli settled a knee on the bed and kissed her, reviving her passion and putting nothing but him and this moment at the front of her mind. "I forgot where I put the box."

She tried to hide her smile but failed. "The box?"

He winked as he came over her. "We're just getting started."

She stared up at him, and her breath caught. He was truly the most beautiful man she'd ever seen, cut and sculpted and obviously ready. For her.

"Eli," she said again.

He looked serious now. Focused. Tucking the condom beneath the pillow at her head, he began to tease and kiss her all over. His lips tugging on her nipples, his fingers stroking her just right. His tongue tickling her and driving her crazy as she began to moan.

Placing his hands beneath her, he lifted her and brought his lips to her center. His beard scruff stroked her inner thighs, in delicious contrast to his soft lips on her clit. The edge of his tongue was rough as he began to stroke her deeply. Again and again he drove his tongue into her. Her legs were shaking, and he lowered her body to the bed. His fingers moved in her now. He licked her again and again until she saw stars and surrendered everything. She was flying and falling, and he whispered the sweetest, naughtiest words she'd ever heard as he came up to kiss her mouth.

Her body was flushed, slick with sweat, when he settled himself against her still-tingly flesh. Sliding a hand under the pillow, he withdrew the condom packet he'd put there. She opened her eyes and watched as he took care of it, unable to look away from him. Taking an audible breath, he shifted and finally began to come inside of her.

She bit her lip and stiffened beneath him. It was uncomfortable, and a lot like when she'd lost her virginity her freshman year. It didn't hurt, though. Not at all. She still tightened around him in a kind of reflex.

He froze. "Are you okay, Caro?"

She did a round of yoga breathing and nodded. "Y-yes."

He sank in a little bit more, and she felt herself stretching in answer.

"You feel so much better than okay," he said.

She knew he was teasing her to get her to relax, and it was starting to do the trick. That and his lips on her neck made her tingle as he began to move. He was completely inside her now, hot and hard, and she didn't feel uncomfortable any longer. She felt amazingly full, and so ready for whatever else he had in mind.

"That's it, baby." He withdrew and sank back inside her. "God, Caro."

She reached up and grabbed onto his shoulders, bowing back as she took all of him. She forced her eyes open and was so glad she had. He looked incredible over her, golden and hard and perfect. Everywhere they touched, and even where they didn't, felt tingly. He bent his head to kiss her again, his mouth firm and demanding, and then braced himself on his arms as he moved in and out of her. Rotating his hips, he accelerated his thrusts and she sobbed as her orgasm struck.

He didn't slow down, but just kept riding her as her climax seemed to go on and on. His big body shuddered and he made the sexiest sounds as he began to come. She held on tighter, finally squeezing her eyes closed as she lost herself in him again.

Falling to one side of her, he held her close and kissed her neck. He seemed to like that, and he always breathed in as he nuzzled her. Their bodies were hot and a little sweaty, but his fresh scent wrapped around her as she caught her breath.

"Eli." She took in a reedy breath. "God."

"Back atcha." His hands ran over her, soothing and arousing at the same time. "I said you couldn't disappoint me."

She turned and snuggled against him, running her fingers over him now. His muscles tensed and his breath hitched and she knew he'd been affected. Pleased. She sure was.

"It's been over three years," she said softly.

He lifted his head and looked at her, his eyes dancing. "Man, I am one lucky bastard."

"Lucky?"

"I don't know what happened three years ago, Caro. I know it shook you up, and maybe you'll tell me all of it. Maybe you won't. I feel so damn lucky you chose to be with me right now."

His words sounded so sincere, his gaze was so steady, she felt tears prick at her eyes.

"You *are* good for me, Eli. You always seem to know just what to say to me."

His brow furrowed as he reached up to brush a tangle of hair off of her forehead. "You deserve something good, Caro.

239

I'm just happy that I'm the guy who put that look on you face."

She flushed and gave him a smile. "What look?"

He tapped her nose with one finger and brought his face to hers. "That look of complete satisfaction."

She couldn't deny it, and wouldn't even want to. "What about you?"

"What about me?"

"Were you satisfied?"

He barked out a laugh. "Are you kidding me? I nearly blacked out there for a minute."

She pushed him onto his back, straddling his thighs. "Hmm, I don't think that's good enough."

His hands splayed over her back, sliding down to cup her butt. "What are you thinking, Cupcake?"

Bending her head to his chest, she flicked her tongue over his nipple. He groaned and she faced him again. "I'm thinking that it's a pretty good thing you have a whole box."

He grabbed her to him and started it up all over again.

Chapter 18

"Meeting at four today, Eli."

Eli blinked at Oliver as he stepped into the Sales Center lobby. He'd just finished a tour, and coming in from the bright afternoon sun was a little jarring.

"A meeting wasn't on the schedule," Eli said.

"Mr. Forbes just called it while you were out. I have to go over to the Institute and tell Jessie. She tends to fall into her research when she's over there and forgets to look at her phone."

Eli just nodded as Oliver hurried out the door and across the street. It was Wednesday, which meant that Jessie was over there and the rest of them picked up the slack.

It seemed odd that Mr. Forbes would call a meeting with only two hours' notice. Eli had noticed a vibe around the guy over the past couple of days, but he'd come to notice that Forbes always looked like he was thinking about a dozen different things at once. Besides, Eli hadn't exactly been on his A game since spending the weekend with Caro.

He ducked into the break room and grabbed a fresh bottle of water from the fridge. As he cracked it open, Rick and Ben Chapman came into the room.

"Hey," Ben said with a lift of his chin.

"Hey, Ben," Eli said. "What's this meeting about, Rick?"

Rick held up his hands. "This is Mr. Forbes' gig, Eli. He wants to bring in the salespeople at the outset, though."

"Tammy will demand a full report," Ben said with a smile. "My wife loves staying home with Raffaella but she's ready to come back."

"How long is she out?" Eli asked.

"Forbes wants her to take all the time she needs, but it'll probably just be a couple more weeks."

Rick smiled at Eli. "Don't worry, Eli. You're not going anywhere."

Eli chuckled. "Hey, I've been pulling my weight."

"Yeah, you have." Rick turned to his brother. "Eli has brought in quite a few families to live in the houses you designed, Ben."

"The green neighborhood is very inviting," Eli said. "Your houses almost sell themselves."

"Almost," Rick said with a smile. "You've been a driving force in that direction."

"Thanks." Eli sat at one of the round tables as Rick made himself and Ben a cup of coffee. "I guess we'll find out what's up at four."

"I have a pretty good idea." Noah Brady joined them and grabbed himself a bottle of water. He sat down across from Eli. "Hey, Eli."

Eli smiled at Jessie's husband. It seemed now that it was clear Eli wasn't after Noah's wife, the guy didn't seem to have any animosity towards him. Everyone knew about him and Caro too, so that clearly helped.

"What is it?" Eli asked him.

"Just something I picked up from a few things Forbes has said over the past couple of weeks."

Eli's radar buzzed as he picked up on what Noah wasn't saying. This had to be about the Active Adult community. Forbes was finally going to announce something. Eli had seen some land marked off on the east side during the first tour he'd taken since coming on at the Sales Center, but when he'd returned and asked Jessie about it she'd told him that was a five-acre plot that her sister's fiancé had purchased. He was putting in a goat farm or a petting zoo or something.

"See you at four," Rick said as he left the break room.

Eli stood and took out his phone, thumbing through to sync his schedule. The newly-added meeting was there, clear as glass.

"I'll see you guys there," he said to Noah and Ben.

He left the break room and headed across the street to the coffee shop. He gave the red-headed kid, Tom he now knew, his order for an Americano and a latte for Caro. As he waited, he texted the info to Bill Chapman.

Tell me everything Forbes says, Bill texted back in a flash.

I can only tell you what he declares public knowledge, Eli returned.

There was a long pause and Eli began to worry that putting off Bill's curiosity wasn't a smart thing to do. Eli might be beholden to Bill, but he worked for Cypress at the moment. He owed Forbes and Rick his loyalty and his discretion.

Just tell me what you can, Eli, Bill finally answered. *I'll call you tonight.*

Eli could almost see the determination on Bill's face as he punched in the letters. He let out a breath to tamp down the frustration he had no business feeling.

Talk to you later, he texted back.

Eli slipped his phone back in his pocket and took his drink from Tom.

"Wow, that's a serious face."

He glanced over to see Caro's friend Becky now waiting for her drink.

"Hey, Becky."

"Something wrong?"

"No. I'm just thinking about work."

"Yeah, the meeting this afternoon." Eli arched a brow and she waved a hand. "Oliver came into the Institute, all in a tizzy about the meeting Mr. Forbes called."

He nodded. Tom handed him Caro's cup and he smiled at Becky. "See you."

"Bye, Eli."

Stepping into the bakery, he found Jane behind the counter. It was almost closing time, so he wasn't surprised to find the place empty of customers.

"Hi, Jane. Where's Caro?"

"Right here," Caro said behind him.

He turned and just the sight of her started to lift him out his odd mood. Not caring that Jane was there, he bent his head and kissed Caro. Her lips moved just slightly against his and he made himself pull away.

"What was that for?" she asked with a smile.

"I'm taking my reward in advance." He held out the latte he'd had made just to her specifications. "For you."

She grinned up at him and that tightness in his chest

loosened a little bit more. "Mmm, thank you."

He sipped his own coffee, keeping his eyes on Caro as she brought her pert little nose to her cup and breathed in.

"You're getting good at this, Eli." She took a sip and smiled. "You know what I like."

He wanted to point out that he knew a whole lot more about her than just how she took her coffee. Since their first time Saturday night, and every night since, he'd learned every inch of her body and just what made her sigh and scream.

"I'm a fast learner, Cupcake."

***

Caro felt a rush of want course through her and she kept her hands on her cup of coffee to restrain herself. He was a fast learner, all right. Saturday night had been just the beginning, to her delight and surprise. They'd spent every night together since, although she'd always dragged herself home to her apartment. She hadn't wanted to leave him or his big comfy bed, but she still had a business to run.

"So you have a meeting this afternoon?" she asked as she led him over to the nearest table.

Eli blinked. "Did Becky tell you?"

She shook her head and sat down. "Jessie. She ran in here

to grab a tray of goodies to take to the meeting."

He raked the fingers of one hand through his hair and sat across from her. "Well, that gives me something to look forward to at least."

She caught something in his tone, a nervousness she'd never seen in him before. He always appeared confident and sure.

"What's this meeting about, Eli?" she asked.

"No clue."

"That's it, then."

"What's it?"

"You're going into a meeting without any preparation." She blew out a breath. "I don't envy you, but you'll hold your own."

"Thanks Caro, but I'm sure I will. I just wish I knew what Mr. Forbes had planned."

She finally reached out and touched his hand. "You're worried about something, and I don't think it's just the meeting."

For a split second he looked like he was going to unload some of the burden he was obviously carrying on his broad shoulders. Then he gave her his trademark grin and the moment was lost.

"I'm just thinking about having you over for dinner."

She wanted to push, but she wasn't in any position to demand he share more of himself. The parts of him he did share—his fun, his passion, a bit of his past—had to be enough for now.

"We're having dinner at your place?"

"Or we can have, what did you say it was last time? Pot roast with your parents?"

She gave a dramatic shudder. "Don't even tease about that."

"Then you'll have to come over for dinner. I'm cooking again."

She smirked. "Again? Mac and cheese from a box and a bagged salad isn't exactly cooking."

"That was Monday night."

"And Tuesday night."

"Okay, okay. I can cook, you know."

"You can certainly heat things up," she said.

He gaped at her and then laughed. "Cupcake, giving as good as she gets. I like it."

She flashed him her own cheeky grin.

"Tell me what you need for dinner and I'll pick it up at the market," she said.

"Meat, potatoes. Maybe onions. Whatever you like."

"Are you giving me lady's choice, then?"

"I always do, don't I?"

A memory flashed in her mind, of the two of them just last night as he'd let her take control of the passion play. "Yes you do."

He smiled and drew out his phone, glancing at the screen. "Okay, you're closed now. I have to go prep…something for this meeting." He stood and bent down to kiss her again. "I'll text you later about dinner?"

She stood and followed him to the door. "Sure."

After he left she locked the door and turned the hanging sign to Closed.

"That boy has it bad, Caro," Jane said as she wiped down a table.

She smiled in her direction. "I'm the one who has it bad, Jane. I'm thinking about him all the time."

"And you don't think he's got that going on?"

"I know he does, but there's something up with his work."

"Who gives a fig about his work?"

"He does. It's been the one constant in his life, I think."

Jane's lips thinned. "That could explain the serious expression that sometimes crosses that ridiculously handsome face."

Caro nodded. "I know something's bothering him."

Jane pushed in a couple of chairs and then faced her. "Well, those scones aren't going to prep themselves."

The savory butternut squash scones they'd debuted for the Fall Festival were proving to be very popular, and the dough needed to chill and rest overnight to get them to bake up fluffy and tall.

"Let's have at it, then," Caro said.

By the time they'd done the prep on the scones and some of the other treats they would bake in the morning, it was after four o'clock. Jane ducked out the back of the bakery as usual, but Caro exited through the front and locked up, setting the alarm with the app on her phone. It wasn't a long walk to the market, but her gaze was drawn toward the Sales Center as she made her way past. Mr. Forbes' impromptu meeting was going on right now, and she was worried about Eli. He was a planner, and it was clear from the way he lived his life that he was most comfortable when he knew what was going on.

Maybe it went back to growing up in foster care. That kind

of life must have made him dread any kind of surprise. Any kind of change he wasn't prepared for.

She realized she cared about him. Maybe she even loved him a little bit. She'd wanted to hug him there in the bakery when he'd looked so troubled. It was like when he'd found her out by the lake that afternoon. Was that just a few weeks ago? It felt like she'd seen a different Eli for so long now. A caring, serious man who wasn't quite the bright shiny charmer he presented. It wasn't all the time, but she felt in her heart that there was more to him.

After greeting Jordy at the counter, she wheeled the two-level shopping cart over to the meat case. She chose a package of lamb chops and a bag of baby potatoes. She'd taken a few cooking classes back when she'd been getting her degree, after all. She could cook, even if she spent her days baking. The asparagus looked perky and fresh, so she added a bundle to her basket. A medium red wine would pair well with the meat, and she put a bottle of cabernet in her cart too.

The market had bundles of fresh herbs in the produce section, and rosemary would be a great accompaniment to both the meat and the potatoes.

"I think that should do it," she said as she wheeled up to

the counter.

"Looks good," Jordy said.

He rang her up and she paid, taking another look at her phone. Four forty-five now. How long would Eli's meeting last? She had no clue. This was just another reason why she loved running her own business. Having nobody else to answer to made the struggles and responsibility so worth it.

"Is that all?" Jordy asked.

She nodded absently, her mind on Eli. Something was bothering him. Tonight she would give him the opening he needed to confide in her, but she wouldn't press him.

Forcing an intimacy that went beyond the sexual was so not what she wanted to do.

Chapter 19

Eli sat at the table as most of the others filed out of the conference room. Mr. Forbes had dropped the bombshell and fielded a handful of questions, insisting that more details would be forthcoming. He was gone in a flash, and now the only other person in the room with Eli was Ben Chapman. The architect looked a little shell-shocked as he ran his hand over his hair.

"Ben, you look floored."

"I have a lot to consider when I start on these plans, Eli. What direction are we going in? Entry-level or luxury? Who the hell knows after that meeting?"

Eli nodded. "The sales staff has to presell the place. I wish I had more info."

"Don't we all. Forbes will tell us when he's ready. I anticipate a lot of emails in the coming weeks." He gave Eli a small smile. "I know my wife is going to have a ton of questions."

"When is Tammy coming back?"

"She's been out for almost two months. I'd love it if she stayed home with the baby forever, but I also know my wife." He laughed a little. "She would go crazy. Not everyone is lucky enough to have your mom there when you get home from

253

school."

"Your mom stayed home?"

Ben nodded, warmth coming into his blue-gray eyes. "My mom was the best, Eli. She was a sweet, soft-hearted woman who I still, to this day, can't see falling for a hard-ass like Bill."

"You're lucky you had her. Did you see your father much?"

"Nope. Bill provided *very* well for me, so it was his money that allowed my mom to stay home. But that was pretty much the extent of my father's involvement."

From what Eli had picked up since coming to Cypress, it seemed like all of the Chapman siblings had similar stories of their childhoods with—or without, really—Bill in their lives.

"I never knew my father," Eli said for no reason he could think of right now.

"I'm sorry, man." Ben's gaze was soft. "You come from a broken home?"

"Broken?" Eli scoffed. "Destroyed, actually. I'm an orphan."

Ben's brows lifted. "That sucks."

Ben's words were simple but hit it squarely on the head. Eli nodded, his throat tight. He pulled his mind from the dark place of his own childhood memories.

"Well, I know Rick wants Tammy back." Eli winked. "Although I like to think I've picked a little of the slack."

Ben smiled now. "You don't seem like a guy who sells himself short."

"Not at all, actually."

"Tammy will be glad to have you here." Ben stood, grabbing up his tablet. "I'll see you tomorrow, Eli."

Eli watched him go and synced what few notes he'd taken on his phone to his laptop's server. He studied his phone and knew he'd have to make that call to Bill. He wished he could have asked Ben how to handle him, but from what he'd learned since working at the Sales Center, and from Ben himself this afternoon, the guy didn't have any more contact with his father than Rick did.

He left the conference room and made his way to the large sales room. Jessie was tidying up her desk but everyone else was gone.

"Where is everybody?" he asked her.

"Rick said we could all take off, since it's almost five o'clock."

"Short meeting."

"Shortest in my memory," she said.

"You ready to go, Jessie?" Noah Brady walked into the sales room. "Hey, Eli."

Eli nodded to Jessie's husband. "Hey."

Noah looked as flummoxed as Ben had, and he knew the builder would have to work with the architect on the plans for the newest community in Cypress. The couple left and Eli closed down his computer.

He wasn't sure what time Caro was coming over, but he drove his SUV back to the townhouse and parked in the garage tucked behind the unit. The house felt empty when he walked into the kitchen. He drew out his phone and made the call to Bill. The man answered immediately.

"Eli, tell me what happened at the meeting."

No greeting, but that was Bill's usual M.O.

"There's going to be an Active Adult community built over to the east side of the property," Eli said.

Bill blew out an audible breath. "So. Forbes finally said it. About damn time."

Eli settled on the couch and leaned back. "You knew."

"Of course, I knew. I've been going down there every few weeks."

"To see your family? Because that's what you've told me."

"Yes, to see my family. And to get with the developers to see what investment opportunities were forthcoming."

Eli thought about what Ben had told him about Bill's particular brand of parenting. Money and pretty much nothing else. He'd paid Eli very well in Boston, hadn't he? He supposed he was lucky in that, since he wasn't expecting any sort of fathering like his kids apparently had.

"I don't have the particulars, and if I did I couldn't tell you," he said.

Bill was quiet for a second. "Yeah, Forbes said you'd settled in at the Sales Center. I hadn't thought your loyalty would shift so quickly."

Eli felt his words like a punch to the gut. "What are you saying?"

"I'm saying I could use you back up here."

The room seemed to shift and Eli straightened. "You want me back at Chapman?"

"Maybe. I could make you my Director of Accounts."

Eli held his breath as the offer sank in. "Shit."

Bill laughed. "I thought you'd like that. You were already my number one guy in account retentions, Eli. You can

2222

schmooze with the best of them. Tell everyone exactly what they need to hear."

A buzzing sound filled Eli's head as his stomach churned. Bill had just boiled his entire career down to bullshit artist.

"Thanks," he muttered.

"So what do you think?"

"Are you serious?"

"I'm always serious," was Bill's answer.

Eli smirked at the phone. Truer words were never spoken.

"I'm committed to working for Cypress, Bill." Eli paused. "For your son."

"Rick won't be happy with me, but he's never happy with me."

"I don't care about your relationship with your kids," Eli bit out. "I made a commitment. To Forbes and to Rick."

"Right, right." Bill was silent again. "Listen, Eli. I'm serious about your coming back up here, but I appreciate that you feel obligated to Cypress."

Eli's lips thinned. He kept the words he wanted to say locked behind them, because if he let loose he would tell Bill just where he could stick his appreciation.

"So," Bill went on. "Think about what I said. I'll get with

Forbes myself, but if you hear anything…"

"If I hear anything I can repeat, you're the first guy I'll call."

"Fine." A loud sigh filled the space after that lackluster word. "We'll talk again soon."

It wasn't a question. "Bye, Bill."

Bill disconnected the call and Eli tossed his phone on the couch beside him. Fucking Director of Accounts at Chapman? The position didn't even exist yet, but he was so perfect for it.

"I'm a bullshit artist, after all," he grumbled.

His doorbell rang and he scrubbed a hand over his face. He had to shake this off. Caro was here and they were going to have dinner. He'd suck it up and put on his game face. She'd said he was good for her, and he was going to be that guy tonight.

As for tomorrow? Who the hell knew?

***

Eli opened the front door, a grin on his face. "Hey, Cupcake."

She reached up on tiptoes and kissed him. "Hungry, Graham Cracker?"

His eyes sparkled and she placed a hand on his chest and pushed.

259

"Step aside, Eli. I've got this."

He closed the door and wrapped an arm around her. "I thought I was cooking tonight."

"You were." She kissed him again, because he tasted so good, and pushed past him. "I grabbed a few things, and I thought we could cook together."

He looked a little startled. "I've never cooked with anyone before."

There was something else under his words, but she chose to take them at face value. And tease him a little bit, too.

"Now, we both know that's not true," she said.

He laughed, and his mood seemed to brighten. "Bring it on, then."

What she'd bought at the market didn't need much time, so she set the groceries on the back counter and came up to him again. "Do you like lamb chops?" He nodded. "Asparagus? Potatoes?"

"That all sounds fantastic."

She placed a hand on his chest again, stroking lightly through his polo before patting him. "Then let's get started. The sooner we eat…"

He growled softly. "Caro, you're too good to me."

As they prepped the chops and cooked the veggies, they seemed to move in sync. He was clearly a guy used to cooking for himself, and she wondered where he'd picked that up.

"So did one of you ex-girlfriends teach you how to cook?" she asked, keeping her tone light as if she didn't want to picture him doing anything with another woman. Even something as innocent as making a meal. It was just too homey.

"Nope." He slid the chops under the broiler. "One of my foster moms loved to cook and we had to help."

"How long were you there?"

"Almost two years. Until I was fifteen." He wiped his hand on a dish towel. "I learned a lot from her."

"She didn't bake?"

"Not like you. Cakes from mixes, though. Cookies from tubes of the stuff."

"Mmm, cookie dough."

He slanted a look at her. "Don't tell me you like that dough from a tube."

"Hey, I'm a red-blooded American woman."

Taking her in his arms again, he dropped his hands to her butt. "Yeah, you are."

She tucked her face into the crook of his neck and breathed

in, letting out a purr of contentment. "So let's get ready to eat."

He gave her butt a slap and released her. "You're a tough cookie."

"I thought I was a cupcake."

He shrugged. "You're a treat, Caro. Let's leave it at that."

She lifted her chin and smiled. "I'll take it."

Dinner was as delicious as she'd hoped, and the wine was delectable. They'd not only cooked together but they'd cleaned up together too. He was clearly used to caring for himself, as his movements were easy and confident. He seemed to like her in his space, though. She knew she felt really comfortable in his house.

"So how was your meeting today?" she finally asked as they settled on the couch with their wine glasses.

"It was all right." He took a sip. "Short."

"A Forbes meeting, short?" She huffed out a breath. "From what I've always heard from Jessie, the guy loves his lengthy meetings."

"From what I've seen so far, too. This was different."

That strangeness she'd glimpsed when she'd first arrived was there again, in the stiffness of his shoulders and the set of his sculpted lips.

"Can you talk about it?"

"Oh, I can talk about it. There wasn't a lot of info, and it's going to be public soon anyway."

It struck her then. What the rumor mills had been churning out in tiny bits over the past few months.

"The Active Adult community," she said.

"Yep. It's official now."

She'd lived in Cypress long enough to know just what went into starting up a new community on the property. She'd seen the green neighborhood go from an idea to an actual village, and knew it took a lot of planning and time to bring it to actuality.

"Will you have something to do with it?" she asked.

What she really wanted to know was just how long he'd be sticking around Cypress, but she wasn't going to ask that particular question.

"I hope so. We'll have information to pre-sell to visitors, of course. Ben and Noah will be the point people on design and construction."

"That will keep them pretty busy."

"And both their wives, too."

"Tammy's coming back?"

"Ben thinks she'll want to jump on this."

"They've been operating without a Sales Manager since Raffaella was born."

Eli's lips thinned again. "He'd like her to stay home, like his mom did."

"Ben was raised in California, right?"

"I think so."

"He does have a granola kind of vibe," she said. "He's laidback, like his brother Jake."

"Jake's wife will be pretty busy too, I bet."

"She's the money mind, so yeah."

He drained his glass and set it down. "They'll be bringing on new investors. Bill and I spoke about that a little while ago."

"Bill Chapman?" This shouldn't surprise her, but he hadn't mentioned his old boss in weeks. "Chapman Financial will have a stake?"

"If Bill gets what he wants."

"You don't seem happy about that."

"Oh, I'm happy for Chapman's investors. Believe me."

"Why?"

He brushed his hair off his brow and settled back. His posture was relaxed but his face was set. She felt the instinct to brace herself for whatever he would say next.

"He offered me a job, Caro. An incredible job back at Chapman."

Her stomach clenched painfully, and their wonderful meal churned inside. "Oh."

"It's not a done deal." He blew out a breath. "I don't even know if I want to consider it."

She nodded, her mind racing with everything she longed to tell him. *Don't take the job. Stay here with me forever.* That last scared the hell out of her, because she knew he just wasn't that kind of guy.

"Well, it's a good thing everything you have here is on borrowed time." His eyes widened and she bit her lip. "It wouldn't take much to settle things, right?"

His expression grew more serious than she'd ever seen it. He was obviously considering Bill Chapman's offer. Of that, she had no doubt. What was there to keep him in Cypress Corners, right? Not his house, his furniture, his damn SUV. Sure as heck not the baker girl he was sleeping with.

"I don't want to talk about Bill tonight, Cupcake."

Cupcake. God, she loved it when he called her that silly nickname.

"Me, neither."

"Then let's go upstairs and quit talking altogether."

She let the heat of his words, of his eyes that now held the promise she knew he could deliver, send her apprehensions crumbling like day-old scones.

There would be time enough to regret her decision to date this guy.

When he left Cypress for good and forgot all about her.

Chapter 20

Eli urged Caro up the stairs and back to the bed she'd helped him pick out. He stripped off her cute Sweet Escape uniform and revealing the real treats underneath. She smelled so good, like the stuff she baked and a subtle scent he knew he would always associate with her. She was a sweet escape for him in Cypress. From the first.

She turned the aggressor suddenly, putting her eager hands on his body until he was as naked as she was. He was hard as a rock, and wanted to be inside her so badly he ached with it. Their conversation downstairs, about one of his foster mothers and about Bill's job offer, was forgotten as she fell to her knees and took him in her mouth. He couldn't think of anything but her hands stroking him. Her tongue and lips caressed his shaft and he braced his legs apart. Running his fingers through his hair, he closed his eyes and arched toward her.

"God, Caro," he groaned. "Damn."

She murmured something he couldn't quite catch and took nearly all of him. His orgasm was coming, pulling everything inside him tight and hot as he moaned her name again. When her hands reached around to grab his ass, he lost it. He somehow managed to remain standing as he came so hard he almost cried.

When he caught his breath, he looked down at her. Her expression was proud, her eyes bright and her delectable mouth in a smile as she gazed up at him. Reaching down, he took her hand and pulled her to her feet.

"You drive me crazy, Cupcake. Do you know that?"

"I try."

He kissed her, running his hands over every inch of her he could reach. Boston and Cypress and the rest of it didn't matter tonight. Tonight he would make love with the girl who made him feel so damn good he could almost believe he was worth it.

He got his lips on her in the big bed, all over her body until she begged him for what he would gladly give her. Her climax was intense, and when he was deep inside her? He was seized with the rightness of it. Something about Caro made him feel emotions he couldn't even name.

After, in the little while they had together before she had to head back to her apartment, they held each other in the soft half-light. The days were getting shorter, even if the daytime hours still brought the heat. This was so nice, and he just reveled in the smell of her skin and the feel of her body pressed against his side.

"How long were you at Chapman?" she asked, her voice

soft and drowsy.

"Three years." He kissed her brow. "Why?"

"Just wondering at that job offer. Were you expecting anything like that?"

"I was hoping for something like that."

She was quiet, and he wondered if she was wondering about his plans.

"I hadn't told him I want it," he said.

"But you do owe him an answer. You've worked for him for three years."

"Three years, yeah."

It struck him then. Three years. That whatever-it-was that made her so sad that day at the lake happened just as long ago.

"Caro, what happened to you three years ago?"

She stiffened, and then let out a breath. "I was engaged. He cheated. End of story."

"Not if you're still upset about it three years later."

She sat up and drew her legs to her chest, grabbing her hair and doing that twist thing as she pulled it over to one side. "He died. In a car crash two weeks before the wedding."

"Shit." He sat up and turned towards her. "I'm sorry, baby."

She shook her head. "He was cheating on me, which I found out at the same time I found out about the car crash. It sucked all around."

He was dumbfounded. First, that she'd lost her fiancé and then discovered that the asshole had cheated on her.

"It's no wonder you're still twisted up about it."

She looked at him, and in the semi-dark her eyes were shiny. "I'm not mourning him, Eli."

"That's good. Isn't it?"

She nodded, biting her lower lip. "Yeah."

He could read people, and he could tell she was sure as hell mourning something. "You can tell me anything, you know. I don't sit at the table under a tree, sipping sweet tea and trading secrets."

That got a small laugh out of her. She took in a deep breath, he'd seen her do that a few times before, and faced him fully.

"I was pregnant, Eli." She closed her eyes for a beat and opened them again. "I lost the baby. That was what I was sad about that day. It was three years to the day."

Eli couldn't manage to get a word out, which was a first in his memory. Damn, that sucked. His heart twisted for what she'd lost.

"Aw, baby," he finally said. "I'm so sorry."

He drew her close and held her as she curled into him. This embrace was something else, too. Completely different from the frantic heat and passion they'd just shared. He realized he wanted to take away her pain, but he was just the guy giving her a little bit of fun in her life. It struck him then. She'd said she'd needed fun when she'd opened her bakery. She must have still been depressed over her loss back then. How couldn't she be?

"I never told anyone," she whispered against his shoulder.

His heart froze, and then began to pound. This was her secret. A heartbreak she'd kept to herself.

"You can tell me anything."

She nodded, not saying anything more. As he held her close, soothing her with gentle kisses that grew in intensity until they made love again, he could guess what was happening to him. He wanted to take away her pain. He wanted to make her smile. Make her laugh. Make her moan. He suspected he might be falling in love with her.

It was a good thing she would head back to her apartment in a little while. Otherwise he was liable to say something to completely change the rules of their arrangement. They were only dating each other. That was true. She knew he wasn't sure about staying in Cypress and she had family here that anchored her in ways he couldn't even imagine.

He'd seen it at the festival. The easy love among all of them despite the fact that she didn't see her siblings or nieces as often as she'd like to. He knew her parents loved her, too. That they'd supported her after the horrific end of her wedding plans. They would have supported her with that more profound loss, but for reasons he couldn't fathom she hadn't told them. Hadn't told anyone before him, remarkable as that was.

She roused herself and kissed him, gazing up at him with those changeable eyes. "Thanks for dinner. And for everything else."

He smiled and stroked her cheek with the backs of his knuckles. "Anytime, Cupcake."

***

One week had passed since the inevitable had smacked Caro right in the face. She was in love with Eli.

That was the only explanation she could come up with for why she'd told him about the miscarriage. She could blame it on the sex, and that he'd nearly made her cry with the pleasure he'd given her. But there was something in him that drew her, almost since that day out by the lake.

He hadn't said anything more about it since, or about the Chapman job offer for that matter. But on those rare times she'd glimpse that faraway look on his face, she'd known he was thinking about heading back to Boston. She shouldn't be surprised. Hadn't she known all along that what they had was just for now?

Luckily, she had plenty of other things to think about, and a very good means to occupy herself with the bakery. Orders had come in for a few cakes and their fall items continued to be very popular. It was October at last, and the mornings and evenings were much cooler and less humid than they'd been just a couple of weeks ago.

She'd gotten in a run this week, something she hadn't been able to rouse the least interest in since sometime in August. Eli had dragged her out with him on Sunday morning, but with his long legs he'd had to slow himself to stay with her. Luckily they'd only run for about an hour and then climbed into the huge tub in his master bathroom. Oh, what that man could do with a handful of body wash.

"There's that expression I've seen on your face a lot lately," Jane teased. "Hmm, I wonder just who put that there?"

"Never mind." Caro wiped down the kitchen counters as they finished up their prep for the next day. "Do you think we've got enough of the biscotti?"

"I can slice and bake more in the morning if we need to."

"Thanks. That should work."

Jane made her way out the back of the bakery while Caro put the few aprons in the bin for the laundry service to pick up in the morning. It was just after four o'clock, so she sat at her little desk in the back and went online to pay the bills. She thought back to when she'd first opened, and how the bills had seemed astronomical when compared to the money coming in. That was no longer the case, thank God, but it would be silly not to keep that in perspective. Things do get better.

She'd gotten over Brad in a heartbeat, and over his cheating almost as quickly. The miscarriage had been much harder on her, and she acknowledged the fact at least to herself, it might have been worse since she'd never shared her loss with anyone at the time.

There seemed to be babies everywhere in Cypress, which she'd seen at the festival. Tammy Chapman's little ravioli was a gorgeous dark-haired cherub and Claire was about to deliver her Baby Chapman any day now. Jessie had only touched on the subject, but Caro suspected that she and Noah would want to add to their family soon. And she'd heard whispers that Harmony and Rick might have something to announce in the coming months as well.

Oliver, funny guy that he was, called it a plague of babies. He and Todd didn't even have a dog together yet, so Caro gave him a pass for his attitude on the subject. They weren't in that place yet, she supposed.

She wasn't in that place either, was she? Nope. Not even a little bit. She was dating a guy with a clear expiration date stamped on his beautiful backside. There was no way she could be thinking about having his pretty blond children.

She gasped and straightened in her chair. An ache settled in her chest, a yearning for something she hadn't even known she'd wanted. It was like when she'd lost the baby. The feeling of mourning something she'd barely had time to recognize before it was gone. It was like that with Eli.

She loved him, not that she would ever tell him. Yet it would be over soon. Of that, she had no doubt. He would go back to Boston and take up his new job. He would return everything he'd borrowed, except her heart. That he would take back with him. No relationship. No love. Sure as heck no baby.

"No future," she murmured.

Shutting down the computer, she tidied up and handled a few last minute things before setting the alarm and heading out back to her car. The yoga studio called to her, so she grabbed her stuff out of the trunk and headed to the four thirty class.

She was just rolling out her mat when Cassie Chapman strolled in. "Hi, Caro!"

"Hi, Cassie. I haven't seen you in a while."

Cassie brushed a thick dark curl off her forehead and sighed. "My brother is a tough customer."

Caro knew that Cassie ran the kids' program out at the Adventure Trails for her brother, Jake. She also knew that the siblings were very close.

"Jake must be getting excited for the baby," Caro said.

"He can hardly sit still! Not that he's much for sitting still."

"How much longer?"

Cassie scrunched her face as she thought. "Maybe a week? I'm not sure." She jumped as her cell phone buzzed. Drawing it out, she looked at the screen and let out a yelp. "Speak of the little darling! Claire's in labor!"

The yoga instructor came in at that moment and Cassie waved a hand at her. "Sorry to run, but my brother's wife is in labor. We have to rally the Chapmans to keep him from losing his mind."

"Give them my best!" Caro called.

Cassie said she would and hurried out of the studio. A few of the women remarked about the blessed event, at which Caro nodded. The yogi began the class, and Caro did her best to move with her breath and follow the postures.

Her mind was so cluttered today, it was tough to listen to her body as she moved. To find her center and focus. Finally, the instructor's soothing voice and the tinkling New Age music began to relax her. By the time the hour was up, she felt decidedly better. Her energy was still scattered though, and her mind took up its circles again as she grabbed her bag and left the Fitness Center.

She checked her phone and saw that Eli had left her a text.

What are you up to, Cupcake?

Smiling, she texted back. *Just got out of yoga.*

Learn a few new moves I should know about?

Feeling those tingles that only Eli gave her, she answered him. *That's for me to know...*

There was a long pause. *I'll be home by six.*

She wouldn't play games with him. Not now. *I'll be there.*

She drove home to shower and dress for dinner and whatever at Eli's house. As she got ready, she thought back to Claire and her coming bundle of joy. She was thrilled for Claire. She really was. She and Jake had tried for a long time to get pregnant, and Caro wished them only the best. Her heart did ache a little bit. She'd made enough space in her body at yoga to recognize that and own it.

Seeing proof of yet another baby didn't make her miss her own lost little angel, though. No.

It made her miss the ones she would never have with Eli.

Chapter 21

Eli was just coming back to the sales room after his last tour of the day when Jessie came flying in behind him.

"Claire's in labor!" she cried. A big smile was on her face. "I knew it. I just knew it!"

"How?"

Jessie stopped for a second, and then waved both her hands. "I don't know. Something she'd said about her back."

"Her back?"

"Oh, good." Oliver came over to them. "I'm not the only one without a clue about this baby stuff."

"But you were in the labor room with Tammy," Jessie said.

A horrified expression crossed Oliver's face. "Only for a few minutes until Ben got there. Girl, please. There was no way I would have stayed."

"You would have if Tammy asked you," Jessie said with a sharp nod.

"Yes, well let's not even think about it," Oliver said.

Eli wondered about all that baby stuff as they argued back and forth. He'd never been around any pregnant women, and he'd always thanked his lucky stars that he'd never slipped up and brought an unwanted child into the world. He'd been one himself, and he was always very careful to never do that to a kid. When he had kids, it would be different.

Whoa. His stomach dropped to his shoes. Where the hell had that come from. Since when did he ever think about having kids? It had to be all the hormones in the air. They were obviously making him nuts.

"Where did they take her?" Oliver asked Jessie.

"The Women's Hospital up in Orlando. That's what Cassie said when she came barreling in here to grab Ben and Rick."

Eli realized then that his boss had left while he'd been out. He'd hoped to talk to him about Bill's offer, now that a week had passed and more info was trickling in about the newest project over on the east side of the property. He wasn't comfortable keeping anything from his boss, especially given the contentious relationship he had with his father. With the arrival of Bill's newest grandchild's imminent, the man would probably be heading down to Cypress soon.

"What's up with the face, handsome?" Oliver asked him.

"Hmm?" Eli looked around and saw that Jessie was gone. "What?"

"You looked about a million miles away, Eli." Oliver gasped. "Don't tell me you're counting weeks in your head."

"Counting for what?" It hit him then. "No, I'm not."

"Whew." Oliver held up his hands. "Not that I'm against babies, but it seems to be an epidemic around here. First Tammy, then Claire."

"That's hardly an epidemic, Oliver."

"Still, once hormones start flying?" He held a hand against his flat abs. "I'm just glad I don't have the equipment."

Eli snorted a laugh. "Oliver, you kill me."

Oliver grinned. "At least the day is over. Leave it to Claire to time it just right. She'd said she put in the end-of-month numbers just yesterday."

Eli just nodded, his mind on the couple of conversations he had to have and soon. First, there was Bill. He had to tell him his decision about the job offer. Secondly, there was Rick. He had to know about it, too. Third? Third was Caro, and he didn't know what the hell he would tell her. About the job and about his feelings.

If his foster placements all had something in common, it was that feelings should never be brought up or dwelled on. He'd learned to suck it up pretty early on. He would just do the same now.

With all the baby talk, he had to wonder if Caro ever

wanted to try again. She was an affectionate, caring person. Everyone only had nice things to say about her, and he'd never met anyone quite like her. Spunky and independent, yet loyal and loving. She would make an incredible mother someday.

Maybe it was well past the time he should have a serious conversation with her. He never made plans. In fact, he prided himself on the talent for always being ready to bounce that he'd cultivated. Living out of suitcases, or backpacks, had given him the skills to roll with the punches. Maybe he had been settling in back in Boston for the last three years. Maybe he had been starting to think about a future at Chapman Financial. That didn't mean he was looking to start that future now.

He and Caro had discussed just what they were doing before they'd even gotten started. They'd agreed to date each other exclusively, which if he was being honest was the first time he'd ever wanted that kind of promise. And it *was* a promise. He knew how to keep promises.

He might not have ever known where he would land when he was being moved from one home to another, but he always promised himself to fit in. To get along with the other kids and to keep the grownups happy. He'd kept those promises too, even if sometimes he was desperately unhappy in a situation.

She was coming over tonight. He would just focus on that and forget about the other two things on his to-do list. He had trouble thinking about anything else but her when she was around anyway. Why would he think about Bill or Rick Chapman tonight?

Her little green car was parked in front of his townhouse, and he saw her sitting on his stoop. He really should get a bench. He caught her attention and returned her wave, and then drove around to the back. He stopped a second to look at their texts from earlier on his phone. He couldn't help but smile. She'd learned a few new moves in yoga? Maybe, maybe not. He could show her a few moves of his own. No hardship there.

She was standing at the door when he opened it, looking fresh and hot at the same time. She'd apparently showered after yoga, and her hair was still a little damp. Wearing jeans and a soft-looking pink T-shirt, she was as tempting as anything in her bake cases.

"Hey, Cupcake." They shared a sweet kiss and he pulled back to see a pucker in her brow. "You okay?"

She blinked and gave a tiny shake of her head. "Sorry. My head must still be back on the mat."

"I've never done yoga, so I have no clue there." She came

in and he shut the door. "How about pizza tonight?"

"Sounds good."

She appeared a little timid, which was something he'd never seen with her.

"Seriously, is something wrong?"

"Hmm? No."

He texted the pizza order to the tavern and put his phone on the counter. "Did you hear about Claire Chapman?"

She nodded. "Class was just starting when Cassie got the call. Apparently all of them were heading up to Orlando to the hospital."

He studied her face for any of the sadness he'd seen a week ago, but he couldn't see it. They talked about nothing much until the pizza came, and he was three slices in when he noticed she'd grown quiet again. There was definitely something on her mind.

"Caro, what's up?"

***

Caro looked over at Eli, reading the concern on his face. She'd caught glimpses of it since she'd walked in, but apparently she wasn't as great at hiding her feelings as she'd hoped.

"Nothing's up, Eli." She wiped her mouth and took a sip of the diet soda he'd bought to keep on hand for her. "I guess I'm tired."

"You do get up at oh dark thirty."

She smiled. "So other than the big Chapman baby news, is anything else up?"

He tilted his head to the side. "You can ask me straight out, Caro. We don't fool around." He smiled a little. "You know what I mean."

She twisted her paper napkin, keeping her eyes down. "I wondered about any new developments." She faced him again. "You know. At work."

"You want to know if I'm taking the job in Boston." It wasn't a question. He had her dead to rights.

Her heart started to flutter and she held up a hand. "I'm not prying, I swear. It's not really my business, we're just dating, but I know you've been on the fence about it."

"We're just dating. Okay." He stared at her and she wriggled in her seat. "I'm thinking of jumping off the fence, yeah."

Her heart sank. That wasn't good. He was going to take the job and go back to the life he had before Cypress. Before *her*. She put on her game face and nodded.

"I think it's a great opportunity for you, Eli."

"You do?"

"Sure. What's the position again?"

"Director of Accounts."

"You would be one of Bill Chapman's right hand guys, right?"

"Yeah."

She'd seen the way his face got when he talked about Bill Chapman. He looked up to the guy. Maybe he even thought of him like a father. Probably more than his own kids did.

"Haven't you wanted that ever since you started there?"

He studied her with those crystal-sugar eyes. "Yeah," he said again.

"Then it's settled."

She brought her soda can to her lips just to do something with her hands, but only pretended to take a drink. She couldn't swallow past the lump in her throat if she tried.

"It's settled?"

"Well, sure! You had the right idea, renting everything here. You'll be able to just pick up and go."

"I didn't rent my bed."

Oh, the bed. "Maybe I'll buy it from you. We made some great memories in that bed."

That got a smile to curve one corner of his mouth. "Tell you what. I'll give it to you. It's a king-size, though. Do you have room in that apartment for a king-size?"

"I can make room, I guess." She chewed a piece of pizza crust, buying herself a few seconds to reorder her thoughts. "You've never seen my apartment."

"No. Now it looks like I'll never get the chance."

"Hey, I saved you from those family dinners," she joked.

He just nodded.

"You said you don't have a clue about how to do family," she went on. "Now you won't have to."

He sat there for a long minute, his face impassive.

"Are you done?" he finally asked her.

Talking? Maybe. Eating? Sure. She looked down at her plate and then nodded. "I guess so."

He closed the pizza box and stuck it in the fridge. Her soda was still sloshing around her can as she tried to look completely unaffected by the ending of their...relationship wasn't quite the word.

She watched him as he stacked the plates in the sink. She wanted to beg him to stay in Cypress. To stay with her. He was halfway out the door, though. She'd seen it in his eyes. He couldn't make connections that lasted, and she wasn't worth the effort of trying.

She hadn't been lying about the memories they'd made in that bed, though. And she would be damned if they ended things without one last roll on that memory-foam comfort.

"Eli?" She approached him and he faced her. "Take me upstairs?"

Heat flared in his eyes. "Wanna take your new bed for a test drive?"

She pressed herself against him. "Oh, yeah."

After he'd loved her with every single part of him, after she'd cried out with pleasure at everything he'd done, she settled against him. She would never forget him. His touch. His kisses. His scent. He was branded on her. She was his.

The really sad thing was, he wasn't hers. He never had been.

Two days later she was in the bakery, about to close up shop. It was Friday, and she hadn't heard from Eli since Wednesday night. Or, as it would always be remembered going forward, their last night together.

Jessie had told her that Claire had an adorable little boy, name to be revealed as soon as new Mommy and Daddy could settle on one. He had his mom's strawberry blond hair, and was a little doll from all accounts. That should come as no surprise to anyone. Jake and Claire would make adorable babies.

She stopped herself when she started to imagine beautiful little blond children of her own. Eli was going back to Boston, or would be soon. It was settled. When Rick came in to buy some biscotti today, on his brother Jake's orders, she'd wanted to ask him about Eli's new job. It would have seemed strange, though. Wouldn't it? She and Rick were friendly but she'd never asked him about Cypress business before.

"I'm out," Jane said. "Great day, boss."

"It was. Thanks, Jane."

Jane stood still for a second. "You know, you can talk to me."

Caro looked into Jane's open, honest face and knew that she could. "It's about Eli."

"I figured as much."

Caro took in a breath. "I got him because he seemed so one-dimensional. I thought I could keep my heart safe by keeping things light and easy, but he's not light and easy. He's deep, damn it. And sweet and I think he's a great guy. I've been wrong before. What if I'm wrong now?"

"What if you're right?"

Oh, what if she was?

"It doesn't matter," Caro said. "He's taking a job in Boston and leaving Cypress for good."

Jane studied her, apparently weighing the wisdom of pressing Caro for more. When she gave a curt nod, Caro knew she had dodged a bullet.

"See you tomorrow," Jane said.

She heard the back door open and shut, and went back there to lock up. She saw that the kitchen was spotless. Bringing in Tom a couple of days a week had been a good decision. Cross-promotion between the bakery and the coffee shop was a win-win, but with him out front with her for the busiest hours Jane could concentrate in the kitchen. It was where she preferred to be anyway. The downside, though? There was a lot less prep work to keep Caro from going home to her lonely apartment.

She kept her gaze forward as she drove past the turn to Eli's townhouse. It was only five o'clock, but Rick usually let the staff go early on Fridays.

Pulling up to her parents' house she saw his SUV was parked at the curb. More than that, she saw him sitting on her ridiculously-small porch. Her breath caught. Why was he here?

To put a period on the end of it for good? She parked and shut off the engine, meeting his gaze through the windshield.

"No time like the present," she murmured to herself.

She got out of the car and he stood as she approached him. He rubbed his hands, he had such nice big hands, on his thighs and offered her a smile.

"Hey, Eli."

He nodded to her. "We need to talk."

Ugh. Were there any uglier four words? "Okay."

She went to unlock the door but his hand stilled hers. "Out here."

"Jeez," she muttered. "Go ahead."

He stared at her, and she figured he could hear her heart pounding in her chest. Her stomach joined the chorus, and she swallowed. "Eli, just say it."

"Just say what?"

"What you came to say!" She took in a breath. "That you're leaving. You're going back to Boston. That you want to measure my apartment for your stupid bed!"

"Easy there, Cupcake. I don't want to say any of those things."

Her head was spinning and she clutched the door handle.

"What?"

"I'm not going back to Boston." He smiled now. "And you sure as hell can't take my bed. It belongs to me, and I'm keeping it in my house."

"So you're staying," she whispered. "That's good."

"You don't sound like you think it's good. I'm staying."

Her heartrate slowed a little. "For now."

He shook his head. "No. Not for now."

She gaped at him, waiting for him to finish what he'd come here to say. "Not for now?"

"Forever."

"You…" She swallowed. "You don't do forever."

He shrugged. "I do now. I called Bill. Told him thanks but no thanks."

"You're not going to Boston?"

He wrapped his arms around her, settling them on her waist. "You're not very sharp tonight, Cupcake."

She found a laugh. "Sorry. This is all a little bit overwhelming."

"Hold on to me for the next part, then."

She grabbed onto his biceps and he grinned. "Go on."

"I'm buying the townhouse. I want something permanent

for once. I want that with you."

"But what about the fence?"

"The what?"

"You told me you made your decision."

"I did."

"You changed your mind?"

"Nope. You assumed I was leaving, and you looked so damn happy about it."

Tears filled her eyes. "I wasn't! Who am I to tell you what to do? Where to go?"

"You're my forever."

A sob caught in her throat. "Oh, Eli."

"Marry me, Cupcake. I promise you won't have to make the cake."

She gave him a wobbly smile. "I love you, you know."

"I know. I love you, too."

She could see it in his face, the truth of his words spreading through her. Letting out a happy cry, she threw her arms around his neck and hugged him tight.

"Well, it's a good thing I bought the big pot roast," her mother said.

Caro sniffled and held herself back from Eli to look at her

mother. "What?"

"Eli called and said he'd be joining us for dinner." She quirked a brow. "He didn't tell you?"

"I didn't get the chance, Mrs. Richmond."

"Now don't stand around outside hanging all over each other." She winked. "You know how the people in Cypress love to talk."

She went in through the front door and Caro turned back to Eli. He stroked her cheek, his thumb brushing over her lower lip. "I love this lip." He nipped at her. "You didn't give me an answer."

"What? Oh! Yes, I'll marry you!"

"And have my babies, Caro?"

She held her breath for a second. "Family, Eli? Are you sure?"

"I think I'm ready. Don't you?"

She just hugged him again.

Epilogue

Eli clicked through his presentation as the people around the table focused on everything he said. Forbes had called another of his famous meetings, and Eli was the point man for the new Active Adults community. Rick had heard from his father what a fantastic job Eli had done at Chapman, and offered him the prime sales position. He would have an office next to Tammy's, now that she was back a few days a week.

Part of his job was to bring everyone on the sales staff up on the latest developments of what would undoubtedly prove to be the fastest growing village in Cypress Corners. He would be a liaison of sorts between the Sales Center and investors, including Bill Chapman himself.

The meeting was soon adjourned and Mr. Forbes smiled in his direction.

"Excellent job, Eli. I look forward to more from you in the coming months."

"Thank you, Mr. Forbes."

Forbes left the room and Jessie winked at him as she passed by. Bree waved and Oliver gave him a fist-bump of all things.

"Will we see you and Caro on Thursday?" Rick asked.

"Yes. It'll have to be after dinner, though. Apparently Caro's family goes all out for Thanksgiving."

"There will be wedding talk, Eli," Ben put in. "I caught Tammy and Claire with their heads together just this morning."

"Never mind." Tammy shoved a hand against her husband's shoulder. "We were just discussing cakes."

Claire was still out on maternity leave, but she came in during the week to touch base and to update her files. Apparently there was no keeping her at home, and Mr. Forbes didn't even bother hiring someone to do her job while she was out. He joked that she was earning the bonus he'd planned on giving her at the end of the year.

Eli closed his laptop and put his things away as the others left the room. Over the past few weeks he'd come to love his job. He worked with people he genuinely liked, and it seemed he was picking up friends as he went along. Bill Chapman was still cordial when they spoke, and had even told Eli how proud he was of him. That had been surprising, but very welcome.

He went straight home to the townhouse and found Caro waiting for him. She lived with him now, against which her parents only put up a token protest. At his urging she'd finally told her mother about her miscarriage, and all of the Richmonds had given her all the support she could ever need.

"Hey, Cupcake."

She came into his arms. "Hey, Graham Cracker. How did the meeting go?"

"I nailed it."

"I never had any doubt."

He kissed her just because he could, and leaned back. "I told Rick we'll be at their place after dinner on Thursday."

"Good. My mother has already started the prep."

"And what are you bringing to the table, Caro?"

She got a secret smile on her face. "Wouldn't you like to know."

He took her hand and they settled on the couch. He'd purchased everything outright over the past few weeks, and realized he liked having tangible property. "I texted in an order of burgers and fries, if that's okay."

"That's perfect." She settled next to him, folding her legs beneath her. "I'm starving."

"Good. You looked a little peaked this morning."

Her eyes widened and she bit her lower lip. She was worried about something.

He cupped her cheek and rubbed a thumb over her lip. "I

love this lip." He kissed her. "Now tell me what's bothering you."

"Not bothering me, exactly."

"Spill it, Cupcake."

"We might have to move the wedding date up."

"I thought you wanted to get married on Valentine's Day. You went on and on about different kinds of pink frosting."

"And you responded by saying just where you wanted to put that frosting before licking it off, if I recall."

He grinned. "Hey, the offer still stands."

"Nevertheless, I think earlier might be better."

"You'll get no argument here. I told you I was all in with this family stuff. Bring it on."

Her eyes brightened and she kissed him hard. Then she stared at him for a beat. "I'm pregnant."

His mouth dropped open, and then a crazy kind of warmth filled him from his belly outward. "Pregnant?"

"We're having a baby, Eli." She bit that lip again. "At least, I hope we're having a baby."

"We'll have this baby." He took her hands in his. "When?"

"Which when? When, the wedding? Or when, the baby?"

"Both. Either."

"Baby, in July. Wedding? That's up for debate."

He threw up his hands. "No argument from me. Get with your mother and figure it out. I want to marry you before our little cupcake starts to rise."

She groaned and then giggled. "That was pretty bad, but I'll take it."

He kissed her and pulled back to press his brow to hers. "I love you, Caro. I'll love our baby, too."

She cuddled against him and he held her as close as possible. It was amazing, really. How his life had changed since coming to Cypress. Yeah, he had a great job. He had friends now, too. But most importantly, he had Caro.

She was his love. His life. His family. She gave him everything he'd ever dreamed of as a kid, and she was his forever.

About the Author

JoMarie DeGioia is a bestselling author of Historical and Contemporary Romance. She's known Mickey Mouse from the "inside," has been a copyeditor for her tiny town's newspaper, and a bookseller. A hybrid author, she also writes Young Adult Fantasy/Adventure stories, New Adult Romance and Paranormal Romance. She gets lost in DIY projects around the house and works out plot ideas during long runs. She divides her time between Central Florida and New England.

Discover other books by JoMarie DeGioia

The Bridgewater Brides series, including

The Heir's Treasure

The Shopgirls of Bond Street series, including

That Determined Mister Latham

The Gentlemen Undercover series, including

A Hero and a Gentleman

The Dashing Nobles series, including

More Than Passion

Pride and Fire

Just Perfect

More Than Charming

The Cypress Corners series, including

Finding Harmony

Taming Jake

Loving Cassie

Winning Ben

Showing Jessie

Seeing Shannon (Barefoot Bay Kindle Worlds Novella)

Dreaming Eli

Giving Chase (Barefoot Bay Kindle Worlds Novella)

Kissing Bree

The Gifted Young Adult Fantasy/Adventure Trilogy, including

Gifted

The Braunachs of the Dell series, including

Luke's Gold

Patrick's Promise

Sexy Historical Novellas, including

In the Baron's Bed

In the Knight's Chamber

Connect with me online

Get the latest news!

http://www.jomariedegioia.com/newsletter-sign-up-.html

Be a VIP Reader!

https://www.facebook.com/groups/529444270572261/

Twitter: https://twitter.com/JoMarieDeGioia

Facebook:

https://www.facebook.com/JoMarie.DeGioia.Author

Website: www.jomariedegioia.com